"All right. Let's get the interview over!"

But as Leigh pulled her tape recorder from her bag, Slade shook his head. "This isn't the right place." He grinned. "In fact, it's a long way from here."

Her eyes sparked resentment. "Would you care to let me in on the big secret?"

He took her arm to usher her to the door. "Oh, it's not such a secret, Leigh. I'll meet you there."

Surely, Leigh thought, he can't mean the island—their island. Angrily she said, "Slade Keller, or Ross Stuart, or whatever you choose to call yourself—I will not play these ridiculous games a moment longer." She wrenched her arm free. "You can wait in your mystery place till hell freezes over—I won't be there!"

"No?" To her utter astonishment, he softly brushed her lips with his. "Something tells me you will, Leigh Daniels."

Scottish born **RACHEL ELLIOT** at the age of six told her primary school teacher she wanted to be "a reporter—because I won't have to do any sums and I'll be able to write all the time." After the training grounds of University, Journalism College, a provincial newspaper and a commercial radio station, she is now a reporter/presenter with Carlisle-based Border Television, which serves Cumbria, the Borders, Berwickshire, Southwest Scotland and the Isle of Man. Her mother and aunt live with her in Cumbria—along with three dogs, two budgies and the fulfillment of a childhood dream—a silver-gray Arab mare, Rhanna.

RACHEL ELLIOT

journey back to love

Harlequin Books

TORONTO • NEW YORK • LONDON
AMSTERDAM • PARIS • SYDNEY • HAMBURG
STOCKHOLM • ATHENS • TOKYO • MILAN

Harlequin Presents first edition October 1989
ISBN 0-373-11207-6

Original hardcover edition published in 1988
by Mills & Boon Limited

Printed in U.S.A.

CHAPTER ONE

THE taxi driver drummed his fingers impatiently on the steering-wheel, casting a sideways glance at the meter ticking steadily on. Either this lady was one rich cookie, or she had an indulgent sugar daddy with a bulging wallet waiting at the other end. Judging by the glimpse he'd caught of her when she popped her head round the door to say she would be ready in five minutes, the latter seemed quite possible. He pushed back his sleeve to look at his watch—twenty minutes and still counting. Not that she wasn't worth waiting for. Even with her hair falling about her face in damp, uncombed tangles, and not a trace of make-up, she had still been a beauty, with a smile sweet enough to melt the sphinx. But he had work to do, and a boss back at base piling up the bookings. Another ten minutes and he would be late for his next call-out, and that was one of his regulars—a businessman who regularly drank too much and couldn't face the rigours of the Tube in the morning. Guarantee him a peaceful drive and he was always good for a hefty tip. No way was he going to lose that little earner to one of the other cabbies, even if the lady was gorgeous. Looks he could find in the cinema.

'Come on, blondie,' he muttered crossly, reaching for his cigarettes. 'I haven't got all day.'

'I'm so sorry driver, have I kept you waiting?'

The voice caught him by surprise and he flinched as the lighter flame hit his fingers. He half turned in his seat to give an equally blistering reply to the woman climbing in behind him, only to find the words dying in his throat. Lord, but she was lovely. The golden hair he had seen earlier in such glorious disarray now curled about a face so exquisite it took his breath away. Almond-shaped silvery blue eyes twinkled apologetically above cheekbones high enough to grace a cat, and the smile on those full curving lips was enough to make him forget the businessman. It wasn't every day angels travelled in his cab.

'Don't give it a second thought, miss,' he found himself saying. 'I didn't mind hanging on a few minutes. Now where would you like to go?'

'To the offices of *She Speaks*. Do you know the place?'

He nodded, recognising the name of the well known glossy magazine. 'An actress, are you, miss? Going to be interviewed, I'll bet.'

Her tinkling laughter sent a delicious shiver up his spine. 'No, nothing like that. I work for the magazine. At least, I hope I still do. My boss is a demon about time-keeping.'

He took the gentle hint. 'Don't you worry. I'll have you there in no time.'

Leigh settled herself in the back seat, hoping the driver wouldn't carry on chattering. The headache she had been trying to ignore since first opening her eyes that morning was fast taking over, and the last thing she needed was small talk. Her own fault of course—she should never have let herself be persuaded to go on to the nightclub—but everyone had wanted to celebrate her latest scoop, and in the end good sense had lost out. Anyway, she had deserved the night out. She had worked hard to track down the story. Whether certain people would ever talk to her again was doubtful, and the thought brought a faint frown to her face. Then she shrugged—it was a story that needed to be brought out into the open, and if that had made life a little uncomfortable for the main characters, then they only had themselves to blame.

'Not a reporter, are you?' The driver's words cut into her reverie. 'Never could stand them myself—real bunch of snoopers. Bet they've all got a few skeletons of their own rattling round, but you never hear about them. No, the Press boys look after their own.'

She let him ramble on, glad she hadn't been pinned down to an answer. Anyway, he was way off the mark. There had been a time, nearly five years before, when the so-called gutter Press would have been only too happy to spread the details of her life across their centre pages. Not because of her—at that stage she had been just another hard-working hack on a provincial weekly, not worth a single column inch to the gossip writers. But they would have queued up to scrabble for the details about the man who had caught up her life in his hands and turned it inside out.

Leigh's silvery eyes grew strangely cloudy as his image came into her mind. She so rarely allowed herself to think of him, yet his face was as clear to her now as if he were standing before her. Tall, broad, with the look of a man used to wide open spaces, amber-brown eyes creasing at the corners when he smiled that lazy smile. Even over the years that smile could still turn her insides to molten butter. He had carried himself with an easy loping grace and authority that had always made her think of a lion. The similarity hadn't escaped the attention of others—he'd become known as the lion of the screen, king of all he surveyed. With her he had been warm, gentle, tender. Until that last bitter day when the lion showed his claws and blazing anger turned his laughing eyes to dark pools of acid fury. It was the last memory she had of him—he had turned from her then, wrenched himself away as though afraid his anger would transform itself into violence. Strangely, she hadn't been afraid, had longed to run after him, begging to be heard, aching to say it was all a terrible mistake. But she had been rooted to the spot, paralysed by the knowledge that there had been no mistake—that there was nothing in the world she could say to put things right, to turn the clock back.

She had never seen him since that day—except a hundred times in magazines, or accidentally on a television screen. But that had been like watching a stranger—a man known to adoring millions as Slade Keller, one of the biggest box-office draws the American film industry had ever had, and a sex symbol craved by women all over the world. The man she had known had been far removed from that unreachable, untouchable screen image. Even his name had been different.

'Here you are, miss.'

Leigh had to drag herself forcibly back to the present as the taxi driver pulled into an empty space at the kerbside and turned to grin at her.

'Hope your boss won't be too hard on you for being late. Just flash him that angel's smile and he'll let you get away with anything. I know I would.'

The thought of old Mother Reilly appreciating her 'angel's smile' very nearly choked Leigh, but she managed to stifle her laughter as she hopped from the cab and paid her fare.

'I do hope you're right,' she said sweetly. 'And thanks again.'

'Any time, sweetheart. Just call.' And he drove away, his broad ruddy face still creased in a grin.

For a second she stood on the pavement watching the cab disappear, a tiny frown puckering her brows. Another smitten male—and all she had done was keep him waiting for half an hour, then let him risk a booking by speeding through the busy streets. Amazing what a reasonably attractive face could achieve—and not just with taxi drivers.

Unfortunately all the glamour in the world wouldn't cut any ice with old Mother Reilly—otherwise known as Christine Bell-Reilly, Editor-in-Chief and all-round gorgon. Ten seconds after reaching her own desk, Leigh was summoned to her office by a secretary who gave her a darkly warning look.

'Go easy. The old girl's breathing fire this morning.'

'So what's new?' Leigh grinned carelessly. She had been on the receiving end of too many Bell-

Reilly tongue-lashings to let another worry her now. So she was a little late—didn't she always meet deadlines on time?

'Just don't say I didn't warn you.' The secretary preceded her into the editor's office, then subsided into her own chair, immediately burying herself in a stack of paperwork.

'Good morning, Miss Bell-Reilly.' Leigh's smile was lost on the editor's broad expanse of tweed-suited back.

'You call this morning?' The swivel chair spun round and Leigh steeled herself not to flinch before the blatant hostility in the piercing slate-grey eyes. It was well known in the building that old Mother Reilly couldn't abide Leigh, who had been the protégée of her predecessor, and would dearly love to dump her along with the piles of unsolicited manuscripts that regularly arrived with the morning mail. Only Leigh's popularity with the readers had saved her skin this far—plus the fact that she scrupulously checked every story she submitted. People might rage and fume at a Leigh Daniels story, but no one had ever successfully sued.

'I'm sorry I'm a little late.' Leigh attempted to look suitably penitent but spoiled the effect with a grin. 'My car's in the garage, not well again I'm afraid. So I had to call a taxi this morning, and of course the blasted thing arrived half an hour late.' She sent a silent apology to the driver.

'Don't bother with excuses, Leigh. I've heard them all before, and most have at least had the advantage of originality. This is the third time you've been late in less than a month. Don't think I haven't noticed.'

'Oh, I know very little passes you, Miss Bell-Reilly.'

The older woman shot her a suspicious look and Leigh mentally kicked herself. She really must stop baiting the old witch, it only got her into deeper trouble. But there was a rebellious streak within her that simply would not bow to bullying.

'I'm well aware you're one of our top writers, Leigh, but that's not enough. I need reliability from my journalists—in fact I demand it. So far you've proved yourself sadly lacking in that department.'

The remark stung. Leigh had never failed to come up with the goods, no matter how difficult the assignment—and she had never missed a deadline. She opened her mouth to hit back with a sharp retort, but changed her mind at the last moment. The old girl might not have right on her side, but she did have the power of her position. No point in giving her more ammunition.

The editor smiled, obviously aware she had touched a nerve. She so seldom managed to pierce the girl's defences—when it did happen, it was like a minor victory in the cold war between them.

'Was there anything in particular you wanted to see me about?' After her tiny slip, Leigh's composure was back in place, her smile as charming as ever.

'As a matter of fact there is.' Christine Bell-Reilly glanced down at a single sheet of paper lying on her immaculately tidy desk. 'Although we wouldn't have needed this private meeting if you'd deigned to turn up in time for the morning conference.'

Leigh gritted her teeth and let that one pass. 'I already know what I'm to be working on next,' she said evenly. 'If you recall, I submitted the idea for an in-depth look behind the scenes of a new religious group operating here in London. They seem perfectly respectable on the surface, but I'm sure there's a lot more there than meets the eye.'

'Yes, yes, I know all about that.' Bell-Reilly sliced into her explanation. 'I've already given that story to Josephine.'

'Josephine?' As a snub, it wasn't even subtle. Josephine Fairley had only been with the magazine for a couple of months. Leigh liked the girl, found her enthusiastic and hard-working, even if she did have an irritating tendency to forelock tugging where the editor was concerned, but she was far too inexperienced to deal with this kind of story.

'That's what I said.' The grey eyes hardened. 'Are you questioning my decision?'

'No, but that is *my* story.' Even though she knew she was fighting a losing battle, Leigh couldn't bring herself to concede defeat.

'There's no law which says any journalist on this magazine will necessarily cover a story she's suggested herself.'

'But I've already given a great deal of thought to the best way of tackling it.' Not to mention the phone calls she had already made to useful contacts, paving the way for meetings with the right people.

'And I'm quite sure Josephine will be quite happy to listen to any tips you might have. Though at the end of the day, of course, it will be up to her to cover the story as she sees fit. Now if you don't mind, Leigh, I have a very busy morning ahead of me, what little there is left of it.' The editor glanced pointedly at the heavy man's watch strapped to her wrist. 'I really hadn't intended wasting so much time on this. I've got another job lined up for you—an interview with an American celebrity visiting Britain.'

'A what?' Anger and amazement battled for room in Leigh's expressive eyes. 'But surely I could do both jobs. A couple of hours to read the biography and any other relevant background material, then do the interview in the half-hour or so these superstars graciously grant us, and I could have the piece on your desk by the following day.' It was the type of job she had done dozens of times before.

Miss Bell-Reilly's lips twisted into a cold smile. 'I think you'll find this one will take rather more work than that. This particular celebrity isn't renowned for his co-operation with the media.'

'Then why can't Josephine do it? If you're so keen to let her get experience, then surely this would be a better job for her to cut her teeth on?'

'Perhaps it would. But he's especially asked for you. In fact he agreed to do the interview on the sole condition that you did it. And it is something of a coup for us, since he's refused to speak to any other magazine, newspaper, radio or TV station while he's in this country.'

The words stopped Leigh in her tracks. For a second she could only stare at the older woman, thoroughly taken aback. It seemed highly unlikely that any American celebrity would ever have seen any of her work, so why on earth choose her?

'Just who is this mystery person?' she said at last.

Miss Bell-Reilly's eyes held more than a glimmer of malicious pleasure. 'I'm not much of a film-goer myself,' she began, 'so I confess I don't know a great deal about the man. But from the reactions of your female colleagues when I told them at conference this morning, I gather he's something of a heart-throb.'

The tiny hairs on the back of Leigh's neck began to prickle. 'Who is he?' she said hoarsely.

Miss Bell-Reilly glanced again at the paper on her desk as though to refresh her memory. 'Rather an odd name, I can't help thinking, but apparently very much in keeping with his macho image. He's called Slade Keller.'

It was only by a supreme effort of will that Leigh managed to remain expressionless in the face of this bombshell—that, and a stubbornly held resolve never to show weakness in the face of the enemy. She thought she discerned a faint flicker of disappointment in the editor's eyes—did the old witch know something of her past history with Keller?

'Why are you asking me to do this story?' Her voice was calm, betraying nothing of her inner turmoil.

'As I already explained, Keller has specifically asked for you,' the editor said impatiently. 'Here, see for yourself.' She thrust the letter she had been holding across the desk. Leigh studied it without picking it up, unwilling to have even that much contact with the man. His signature at the end of a couple of typed paragraphs leapt out at her, bold, black and sprawling—the mark of a man in a hurry to be elsewhere. She scanned the page quickly—it wasn't so much a request as a command, phrased in a terse, abrupt style, leaving the reader in no doubt that he meant what he said, and would accept no alternatives.

'What happens if I refuse?' Leigh dragged her eyes from the paper.

Bell-Reilly shrugged. 'It's quite simple. If you refuse, then I'll simply suspend you till you come to your senses.'

Leigh knew the woman was serious. This was just the opportunity she had been longing for—to oust Leigh from the position she had so carefully carved for herself at the magazine. As long as Leigh did all that was asked of her, the editor had no good reason to get rid of her—but if she refused to do this assignment, Bell-Reilly could keep her under suspension for as long as she chose. She could leave the magazine of course, but the editor wasn't without influence among her peers, and Leigh had no doubt she would take great delight in blackening her name. In any case, she balked at the prospect of letting the enemy win so easily. But the alternative was to go through with the job—to meet again the man who had broken her heart and left an imprint like a brand on her soul. The years had dulled the pain, but seeing him again could make it flare up all over again, and she wasn't sure she could handle agony like that twice in one lifetime. It would be like walking voluntarily and without any form of defence, straight into the lion's den. Yet—could she really give up the chance to see him again? After all the nights she had spent longing for him, aching for the sight and touch, even the very smell of him—was she really strong enough to turn away from this? Even though it could only lead to all the old wounds being re-opened, Leigh knew this was the strongest argument of them all. She took a deep breath and faced the editor, unconsciously squaring her shoulders for the battle to come.

'I'm not happy about this,' she said evenly. 'But I'll do it.'

Bell-Reilly's eyes gleamed. 'Somehow I thought you might.'

'I'm here to see Mr Keller.' Leigh wondered if the tremor in her voice was apparent to the cool blonde at the hotel reception desk. 'He is expecting me.'

'Ah, yes. Miss Daniels, isn't it? Mr Keller asked me to send you up to his room as soon as you arrived.'

'To his room?' She hadn't expected that. 'Couldn't you ask him to come down here? I'm sure we could talk over a cup of coffee or something.'

The blonde girl shrugged. 'I'll call his room and ask if you like.'

She moved to the switchboard and Leigh leaned against the reception desk, suddenly needing its sturdy support. Just what kind of game was he playing? She had managed to reassure herself that she would be safe with other people around to witness their meeting—that he'd never make any kind of a scene with an audience present. She hadn't considered the possibility of being alone with him, and the prospect frankly terrified her.

'I'm sorry, Miss Daniels, Mr Keller insists you go to his room.' There was more than a hint of a supercilious smirk on the receptionist's carefully pencilled lips. 'He says he's already ordered coffee from room service.'

'Very well.' Leigh took a deep breath, determined not to let the other woman know how she was feeling. 'If you could just give me directions.'

In the lift she gazed at her own reflection in the full-length mirror on one wall. When Bell-Reilly had told her the meeting with Keller had been fixed for that afternoon, she had persuaded one of the magazine drivers to take her home to change, unable to face seeing Slade in the fashionably short leather skirt she'd been wearing that morning. Instead she had chosen a dark grey jacket, tailored to fit snugly at the waist, and a matching pencil-line skirt ending just below the knee. High-heeled grey leather boots gave her extra inches, but she knew he would still tower over her. A vivid scarlet shirt completed the outfit and gave colour to a naturally fair complexion that today seemed even paler than normal. Striving for an efficient, no-nonsense look, she had pulled her riotous golden curls into a loose top-knot, feeling a pang for the times he had run his hands through her hair and whispered soft words into it. Because he'd once told her he preferred to see her without make-up, she had deliberately used more than her normal light covering, but it only served to enhance her delicate features. All in all, she decided despairingly, she looked like a frightened waif, dressed up in someone else's clothes. For a lot less than two pins she would have turned back even now, cut and run, even if it did mean losing the war with old Mother Reilly.

Then the lift doors slid back and her heart thudded into her boots as she came face to face with the man who had haunted her dreams for the past five years. Her first conscious thought was that he hadn't changed—leaning casually against a wall, he was even dressed in the same sort of clothes he had worn back then, snugly fitting faded blue jeans that moulded to his long legs and narrow hips, and a red tartan shirt stretched across a broad expanse of chest. For a second she was mesmerised by the soft dark hair revealed by the shirt's open neck, the sight triggering a rush of memories.

'Well, hello, moonlight lady.' The softly drawling voice dragged her back to her senses and she raised her eyes to his face, almost afraid of what she would find there. Now she could see faint traces of what the years had brought to him—there were lines at the corners of his eyes not etched there by laughter, and shadows lurked in his tawny brown eyes that had never been there before. But when he grinned the shadows vanished, leaving her unsure if she had simply imagined them.

'Hello, Slade.' Her words were stilted, betraying her uneasiness, and his eyebrows lifted in mock surprise.

'Slade?' he echoed. 'What happened to Ross? Or had you forgotten my real name?'

Forgotten? How could she forget the name she had whispered so often into that hard, muscular chest, had cried aloud in the cover of darkness when she awoke to find his crushing embrace had been nothing more than a dream?

'I'm here to see Slade Keller, not Ross Stuart,' she said crisply, terrified of the emotions clamouring within her, begging to be set free. Just two steps forward and she could be in his arms, and only sheer dogged willpower kept her standing still.

His lips twisted cynically. 'That's just what I thought you'd say. So nothing's really changed, has it, Leigh? It was Slade Keller you wanted five years ago. Ross Stuart just got in the way for a little while.'

She shook her head helplessly, but refused to voice the denial that sprang to her lips. The only way she could hope to get through this was to stay impersonal, to keep the man she had known as Ross at arm's length.

He stared at her for a long moment, as though searching for something in her face, and she suffered his scrutiny, feeling she was somehow on trial.

'Come on, then,' he broke the silence at last. 'I've had coffee sent up to my room. Or there's a drinks cabinet if you'd prefer something stronger.'

'Coffee will be just fine, thank you.' Lord, she sounded like someone's prim maiden aunt, she thought irritably, following him along the corridor. His rooms gave her another pang. It was a typical hotel suite, elegant but anonymous, yet he had managed to stamp his personality on it, with clothes strewn over a chair, a pair of tooled leather boots on the floor, a belt with a heavy silver buckle coiled on the low coffee-table. She half expected to see a saddle propped against the wall, and the thought made her smile.

'You haven't grown any tidier, I see.' It was an unguarded remark and she instantly regretted it, but his grin warmed her right through.

'So you haven't forgotten everything after all,' he said softly. 'I was beginning to wonder if I'd imagined it all.'

Unable to cope with the unexpected tenderness in his whisky-coloured eyes, she moved to the table, busying herself with the cups.

'How do you like your coffee?'

'Just the way I always did.' He was challenging her now and they both knew it. She hesitated, feeling his eyes on her, then gave in, adding three spoonfuls of sugar to the strong black coffee in the cup.

'Why didn't you want to come up to my room?'

The question caught her by surprise and her hand trembled as she lifted the saucer from the table. He took it from her, his fingers brushing against hers, and the accidental touch sent a ripple of flame coursing right through her.

'I simply thought it would be easier for us to meet in a public place,' she said carefully.

'Easier for who?' His eyes never wavered.

'Well, for both of us really.' She tried to laugh, but the sound was hollow, unconvincing. 'After all, it has been a long time.'

He nodded slowly. 'Were you afraid?'

Her eyes widened. 'Afraid? No, of course not. What should I have been afraid of?'

He shrugged. 'Not a thing. Unless it was of being alone with me.' He moved closer, bending slightly towards her, his warm breath whispering through her hair. 'You see, I've got a good memory too.' The softly murmured words were like a physical caress. 'Maybe a lot better than yours. I remember the way we once were with each other. I remember the way you used to melt away when I touched you, the way you turned to liquid fire in my arms.' He hadn't touched her, but his words were having the same effect as those long-ago caresses, turning her bones to jelly, robbing her of the power of speech. She desperately wanted to move away but was rooted to the spot, pinned like a butterfly under glass. 'And I remember what we used to do whenever we found ourselves in a room with a bed in it.' He laughed softly, taking her cup from her nerveless hands, and setting both saucers back on the tray. 'Only we didn't always need a bed, did we, Leigh? Remember that time by the river when we had only the birds and the river creatures for company? Do you remember the way the winter sun beat down on our naked bodies and the way you cried my name to the blue sky? Do you remember, Leigh?'

She swayed towards him, mesmerised by his voice and the pictures he was creating in her fevered mind.

'Don't do this to me,' she whispered.

'Don't do what—don't remind you of the passion I can command in you? Has anyone else ever managed to make you feel like this, Leigh Daniels?' With a single swift movement he cupped his hand behind her head and pulled her unresisting body against his, laughing softly when she whimpered in protest. His thumbs stroked stray tendrils of hair back from her temples and tongues of fire snaked through her skin as he bent his head to nuzzle against her throat. Driven now only by the blind need he had always triggered, she tipped her head back, groaning as his strong hands crushed her to him, her breasts flattening against the rock-hard wall of his chest, his thighs pressing into her. Her hands went of their own accord to his shoulders, and when he raised his head from her throat, her lips were parted, her eyes glazed in longing.

'This is how I remember you best, Leigh,' he said huskily. 'Sweet and luscious and ready for loving.' Then his lips found hers and nothing else existed but the man and the power he had never lost over her. Other men had held her since this one, other men had kissed her and tried to stir her to life. None had succeeded and she finally understood why. In this man her soul found its mate, her body recognised its only partner, and she was free to drop her defences and simply rejoice in the sweet fulfilment only he could give.

His lips played gently with hers at first, nibbling softly, planting tiny feather-kisses that left her thirsting for more. Then his kiss deepened, his tongue snaking into her mouth, forceful, demanding, taking what rightfully belonged to him. A large searching hand swept a burning path beneath her jacket to claim one breast, teasing the nipple through the thin, silky material of her scarlet shirt. Impatient with even that slight barrier, he undid the buttons and pulled back the delicate lace of the camisole beneath. When his fingers found her naked skin she gasped, tearing her mouth from his to savour the sweetness of his touch. She rested her head against his shoulder, her senses whirling, the only reality left those questing fingers bringing to life so much that had lain dormant since they had last touched her skin.

'Oh, sweet heaven, Ross,' she murmured. 'It isn't meant to be this way.'

The sound of his name broke the spell. He took a deep juddering breath and gently but firmly pushed her away to arm's length, looking down at her with an expression she couldn't begin to understand. Confused, she began to speak, to ask what had gone wrong, but he stilled her words.

'You're right,' he said. 'It isn't meant to be this way. There's no such person as Ross Stuart as far as you're concerned. He was left behind a long long time ago. And in any case, he's not the one who asked you here today.'

'But Ross, I...'

'No, Leigh. Let him rest. Maybe he never really existed at all—any more than the girl he thought he knew then did. It was all a fantasy, wasn't it? Two people playing out a game, each pretending to be something other than who they really were.'

'It wasn't pretence for me,' Leigh murmured sadly.

'No, you're right again.' His eyes grew hard. 'With you it was just a downright lie. And it seems you were willing to do the same thing all over again—to use that sweet body of yours to get what you wanted. Only it was never Ross Stuart you really wanted, was it, Leigh? Never the real man behind the famous face. No, you only ever wanted Slade Keller—any way you could get him. Well, this time you really didn't have to bring yourself so low—it wasn't necessary. I've promised you an interview and you'll get it. I just wish you hadn't been so eager to sell yourself for it.'

CHAPTER TWO

FOR long seconds Leigh could only stare at him, her eyes beseeching him to understand all she couldn't put into words. Every fibre of her being ached to reach out to him, but the fear of being rejected all over again was too strong.

'Ross, I...'

'The bathroom's over there.' He spoke softly, but there was no warmth in his voice. 'Why don't you go and freshen up? You look a mess.'

His words were like a cold shower. Horrified, she glanced down, only now realising her dishevelled state. With a muffled sob she turned and stumbled from the room, biting back on the tears that were threatening to flow.

'How could you do it, Ross?' She gazed at her reflection in the mirror as if it could give her the answer. 'Why did you want to humiliate me?' Because a long time ago, you humiliated him. The words echoed in her mind and she shook her head in angry denial. She had never intended to hurt him—it had all been a terrible misunderstanding. But even as she whispered the words, she knew it wasn't the truth. There hadn't been any misunderstanding—she had deliberately misled him, tricked him into believing a lie. By the time she'd realised how deeply she was falling in love with him, she was afraid to tell him the truth, afraid she would lose him. Well, she had lost him all right, and that cold-eyed man standing in the next room was more of a stranger now than any of the anonymous faces hurrying by on the streets far below.

'Are you going to be in there all day?' The impatient voice through the door made her jump and she quickly set about repairing the damage caused by those few moments in the next room. Returning to face him was one of the hardest things she had ever done, but somehow she managed to hold her head high, knowing it was the only way she could get through the ordeal. Now the interview was the last thing on her mind—Bell-Reilly could rot in hell along with her blasted magazine. All Leigh wanted was to escape with as much dignity as she could muster, from something she should never have allowed herself to get into in the first place.

Ross was standing by the drinks cabinet when she re-entered the bedroom, a glass of whisky in his hand.

'Well, look at you, Miss Bandbox-perfect. Who would ever have guessed that just a few moments ago you were in my arms, all but begging me to take you?'

She flinched at the undisguised sneer in his voice, but held his eyes steadfastly. 'I think I should go now.'

'Go?' He looked at her quizzically. 'Go where?'

'I think I should leave,' she said patiently. 'I'm obviously achieving nothing by being here. And frankly I don't think it would do either of us any good if I stayed.' She moved to the coffee-table to collect her discarded handbag, but he was at her side in an instant, his long legs crossing the room in a couple of strides.

'But you haven't got what you came here for.'

She looked up at him, stabbed to the heart by the sheer disdain in his tawny eyes. 'I don't think it was ever your intention that I should,' she said with a calmness she was far from feeling inside. 'I think you simply wanted to get me here for some kind of revenge. Well, you've succeeded, so I'll go.'

'Not so fast, Miss Daniels.' His hand snaked out to trap her wrist. 'I agreed to do an interview. I take it you must realise that's not something I do very often.'

'I'm fully aware of that fact.' Everyone in the media world knew Slade Keller was notoriously difficult to pin down. Over the past five years he had punched out more than one reporter for simply daring to try. 'But I really don't see what that's got to do with me.' His fingers were burning into her flesh like a branding-iron, but she made no attempt to shake him off. The last thing she needed now was to antagonise him further.

'I thought you called yourself a journalist, Miss Daniels,' he said mockingly. 'Would you really be worthy of the name if you were to give up on such a brilliant scoop so easily?'

'Is that how you see yourself, Mr Keller?' Her anger was beginning to rise now, try as she might to bite it back. 'I can't help thinking that's a somewhat inflated view of your own importance. Oh, I accept you're Mr Wonderful at the box office, and Mr Superstar to all your fans. But I can't help asking myself, has the well publicised reticence over the years been there to protect you from something, or has it simply been that you haven't had anything worth while to tell?'

'You're the journalist,' he said softly, releasing her wrist, and walking back towards the bar. 'You find out.'

Leigh stared at him, dumbfounded. 'You mean you still want me to do the interview? Even after what's just happened?'

His eyebrows rose questioningly. 'Did I miss something? As far as I'm concerned, nothing happened here at all.'

'Nothing except that you half raped me.' She instantly regretted her hot words, all the more so when a slow smile spread across his sun-bronzed features.

'I did what? Come on, Leigh, I thought you were supposed to be the wordsmith here. Don't you know journalists are supposed to make at least a vague attempt at accuracy? That was no half-rape, lady—as I recall, that was one very willing woman in my arms.'

His words brought a stinging heat to her cheeks, made all the worse because she couldn't even deny them. If he hadn't put a stop to what had been happening between them, they would probably be making love right now. Even in the midst of her anger, the thought made her stomach muscles clench in loss.

'No, Leigh, all I was doing was running a check over your credentials,' he continued unhurriedly. 'As I recall, you weren't too quick to produce your Press card last time we met, and I still haven't seen any sign of it today. I had to make sure I was talking to the right girl, now didn't I?'

It was a low blow and they both knew it. Leigh gazed at him helplessly for a moment.

'Just what do you want from me?' she said at last. 'If you simply wanted to humiliate me, you've already succeeded. Aren't you satisfied now?'

'Satisfied? Hell, I won't be satisfied till I see that article spread right across the centre pages of your magazine.'

'Then I'll ask my editor to re-assign the interview to someone else, since it's obvious there's no way we can ever work together.' Again she turned to go, but again his voice stopped her in her tracks.

'I said you had to be the one to write it, and I meant it.'

'But what's the point?' She turned on her heel to look back, her silvery blue eyes wide with appeal. 'It won't work.'

He shrugged. 'Suit yourself. But I won't do the interview with anyone else.' His eyes glittered strangely. 'And something tells me no editor in his right mind would want anything to do with a journalist who'd backed off from an exclusive like this one.'

Leigh dragged her eyes from his face, looking down at the floor as though she could actually see the gauntlet he had just thrown. He was dead right, of course. If she refused to do the job, it could ruin her career, not only on her own magazine but with every other publication of its kind. Her professional reputation would never withstand the blow. But after all that had happened between them, both in the past and in the last few minutes, could her emotions stand the strain of any more battering?

Slade Keller stood watching, fully aware of the battle raging within the beautiful woman just a few feet away.

'Come on, Leigh,' he said softly. 'What's the choice? You've got everything to gain by doing the interview.'

'And everything to lose if I don't.' She swept her head back, sparks of resentment flaring in her eyes. 'All right, you win. Let's do the damn interview and get it over with.' She pulled a small tape recorder from her bag and looked about her for the best place to sit. But his next words knocked her off balance all over again.

'No, Leigh. That's not the plan at all.'

'What?' Near the end of her tether, she all but spat the word at him.

He shook his head. 'This isn't the right place. Before I do any interview, the atmosphere has to be just right, and it's not right here.'

'So where, then? Downstairs? In another bedroom perhaps? I'm sure the management would be only too willing to give you the run of the hotel.'

He grinned lazily, amused at her petulance.

'The place I've got in mind isn't anywhere in this hotel at all,' he said slowly. 'In fact, it's quite a long way from here.'

'Would you care to let me in on the big secret?'

'Oh, it's not such a secret.' He moved across the room to stand beside her, and took her arm to usher her to the door, ignoring her protest. 'Just give it a little bit of thought, Leigh. I'm sure you'll work it out. I'll meet you there.'

'Slade Keller, or Ross Stuart, or whatever the hell you choose to call yourself—I will not play these ridiculous games one moment longer.' She wrenched her arm from his grasp and whirled round on him. 'You can wait in your mystery place till all Hell freezes over. I won't be there.'

'No?' To her utter astonishment, he dipped his head forward and softly brushed her lips with his own. 'Something tells me you will, Leigh Daniels. Something just tells me you will.'

She drove home on automatic pilot, too dazed by anger to pay much attention to what was going on around her. She would gladly have driven straight to the offices of *She Speaks* to slam her resignation down on Bell-Reilly's desk. But the editor had left on an early afternoon flight for Paris, where she was due to attend a fashion conference.

Back in her small but comfortable flat, she slammed the door shut, wishing it had been on to Slade Keller's head, and took the telephone off the hook. For the next few hours she needed peace and quiet—time to think, and to get her crazy mind back into something like order. Since she always did her best thinking in the bath, she drew a good hot one, recklessly throwing in a generous handful of the horrifyingly expensive bath salts some besotted suitor or other had given her just the week before. The very fragrance of the water made her feel better, and she slid into the warm, silky depths with a grateful sigh, closing her eyes to savour the feeling as the tension slowly began to ease from her body.

On the way home she had sworn wild horses wouldn't drag her to follow Keller, and that she would rather be roasted on a spit than see him again. Now she wearily acknowledged that it couldn't be as simple as that. And it wasn't just because of the interview, no matter what Bell-Reilly, or Slade himself, might think. True, it would do her professional status no harm at all to bring it off, and it would be enough to ensure her place on the magazine for as long as she wanted it. Old Mother Reilly would never dare fire her after the boost in circulation the story would guarantee. But that was less important than the overall need to get this thing with Slade Keller over and done with once and for all. Five years before he had left her life in tatters, and for a long time afterwards she had been haunted by memories, thoughts of him triggered by the most ridiculous things. She had seen friends go misty-eyed at the sound of a particular song and had smiled in sympathetic understanding. But she hadn't needed music to remind her. The aroma of frying onions had once been enough to bring her to her knees, the sight of sunlight sparkling on water enough to catch at her throat, the sound of a dog whimpering more devastating than a knife straight through the heart. Burying those memories deep in her heart had been the hardest thing she had ever had to do, but now she was forced to wonder if she had done the right thing. She had researched and written enough articles on the destructive powers of grief to know that trying to lock the hurt away was the worst possible thing a person could do. Looking back now, she wearily acknowledged her own mistakes. She should have ridden with the pain, allowed herself a period of mourning for something that had died. Perhaps that way she would have got it all out of her system. Instead she had been left with scars and wounds too easily re-opened. And where Ross Stuart was concerned she was still as vulnerable as a new-born kitten. That had been all too clearly proved by the humiliating scene in his bedroom that afternoon. She groaned at the thought of how easily she had fallen into his arms, filled with self-disgust at her own weakness.

The water lapped against her naked skin, as warm and sensuous as his hands had been, and her breathing grew ragged with the thought of his hard body pressed against her, her mind winging back to those long-ago caresses when his lips had traced her every curve and contour, his tongue had explored her every secret inch. Her hands crept up to her shoulders and she hugged herself against the bitter frustration of his not being there to hold and touch, her body aching to experience all over again the storms of passion he had been able to ignite so easily.

At last she opened her eyes, shaken by the intensity of her almost forgotten need. As her heartbeat slowly returned to normal, a tiny ironic smile played about her lips. He had accused her of being willing to use her body to get what she wanted. In his mind she was little better than a prostitute—with the sole difference that she would sell herself for a story rather than for money. If only he knew the truth—that in his arms she became incapable of any form of rational thought, let alone that kind of cold calculation. And how would he react if she told him there had been no one else since him? Her eyes grew wistful. He would never believe it. Five years was a long time for anyone to go without any kind of loving, and there hadn't been any shortage of men willing to fill the empty space in her bed. But something had frozen over deep inside five years before, and though she still enjoyed the company of various male friends, she had never been able to let things go any further. Perhaps that, more than anything else, was the legacy Ross Stuart had left her—to be incapable of opening up her heart to any other man. But perhaps the time had come for her to confront that, because if she didn't, she could go through the rest of her life alone. It was a lonely and bleak prospect.

Immersed in her thoughts, she stepped out of the now cool bath water and belted a long rose-coloured towelling robe about her slender waist. Absent-mindedly she picked up the clothes she had strewn on the floor earlier and took them to the bedroom wardrobe. She wouldn't need them where she was going.

The thought stopped her in her tracks. Somewhere along the way without consciously realising it, she had made her decision. For reasons she couldn't fully explain, even to herself, she was going to follow him. She was going to track the lion down, and see this thing through, once and for all.

CHAPTER THREE

LEIGH gazed out into the darkness as the London-Glasgow train sped on through the night. Around her people were dozing fitfully, curled up in various uncomfortable positions, but though she was tired, she couldn't sleep. It occurred to her that Slade might even be on the same train, dressed in one of the disguises he was so clever at affecting when he wanted to stay incognito, but she dismissed the thought. He would doubtless have chosen to fly north; no rattling around in a train for hours on end for him. She had never had any doubt of his destination—really there was only one place he would choose to go, and her stomach clenched at the thought of it. She hadn't been on the island for five years, though it had once been her favourite place on earth. But after her time there with him, she had sworn she would never go there again, convinced it could hold only painful memories. Now she started to wonder about it—would it have changed? Would it still be the same quiet unspoiled little paradise she had loved, or would it finally have fallen under the hand of commercialisation?

She relaxed back against the seat, letting her eyes close as her mind drifted back over the events that had first taken her to the island. Just twenty-three years old, and working for a small Scottish newspaper, she had been a bundle of energy and ambition then, always searching for the elusive scoop that would lift her from the drudge of provincial journalism to the fast lane of Fleet Street. Finding out about Slade Keller's visit to Scotland to trace his ancestral roots had been an incredibly lucky break—or so she had thought at the time. Yet she had almost missed out on it altogether.

'I want you to cover Arran for a couple of weeks to let the regular chap there have a bit of a break,' her editor Bill Grant had told her. 'And see if you can dig up anything more exciting than he usually sends us.'

'Arran?' She had looked at him in amazement. She knew it was part of the newspaper's patch, but frankly had never bothered to read any of the stories featuring the island. 'The only thing I know about the place is that they knit sweaters there. Doesn't sound like a hotbed of scandal and intrigue to me.'

'Well, for a start, Miss Know-all, it's not where they knit sweaters. For your information that's Aran with one "r", and it's somewhere off the coast of Ireland. The place I'm talking about is a lot closer to home—and anyway, you should damn well know where it is. Didn't you do geography at school?'

She shook her head cheerfully. 'Nope. At least, if I did, no one ever told me about Arran—with one or two "r"s.'

'Well, all the more you'll have to find out for yourself,' the editor said heartlessly.

'But why me?' The prospect of being sent to some God-forsaken plot of land floating somewhere in the sea was as appealing as an attack of toothache.

'Couldn't I do something really exciting for once—like cover the big murder trial at the High Court in Glasgow? You know two local men are involved?'

He laughed. 'Yes, I do know, thanks very much. But I've already promised that job to Niall. It's more in his line.'

'Because he's a man, you mean?' Leigh's eyes narrowed. 'That's unfair.'

'It's also life.' The editor looked at her, a faint trace of apology in his brown eyes. 'Sorry, Leigh, but I feel Niall's the one for the court job. Anyway, look on the Arran assignment as a challenge.'

'Sure. It'll be a real challenge trying to get some sparkling exclusives out of a bunch of sheep.'

'I believe the island is inhabited,' Bill said drily, but not without sympathy, recognising the very real disappointment in the girl's expressive eyes. She was a real go-getter, this one, and he had no doubt she would go far. But he was determined to make sure she could walk before she tried to run. 'Look, if you can find some good stories on Arran, then you'll really be able to call yourself a reporter. Any old hack can follow up on someone else's lead—but it takes real skill to find the stories in the first place.'

Leigh shrugged her shoulders and gave him her sudden beaming smile. 'OK, boss. You never know, I might even surprise you by bringing back a front-page splash.'

He grinned, relieved. 'Knowing you, I'd expect nothing less.'

She had only been on the island for half a day when she got wind of Slade Keller's presence there.

She was sitting in a café overlooking the beautiful broad sweep of Brodick Bay, gazing dreamily at the mountain known as Goatfell, and wondering where on earth she should start in her quest for stories, when a conversation at the next table made her ears prick up.

'Apparently he's here tracing his family roots.' The voice was lowered, but every word carried clearly to Leigh. 'Seems unlikely to me, I must say. I was born and brought up here, and I've never heard of any families called Keller.'

'Perhaps that's not his real name, then,' came the answering voice. 'You know what these film stars are like—look at Marilyn Monroe, she was born Norma Jean somebody or other. Where's he staying then?'

'I'm not sure. I have heard he's over Lochranza way, but it's all gossip of course.'

'Well, if it's true, let's get him along to talk to the Women's Institute. It would make a rare change from flower arranging!'

The two women moved on to another topic then and Leigh tuned out, her mind buzzing with what she had just heard. A film star by the name of Keller here on Arran? That could make a reasonable tale for the paper. But who on earth was he? She racked her brains for a moment, then her eyes widened as a name clicked into place. Slade Keller? *The* Slade Keller, man of her own dreams and a million other women's? It couldn't possibly be. Could it? If it was, and she managed to land an interview with him, it would make a lot more than a few paragraphs in her own paper—the story would be pounced on by any one of the big tabloids. Her mind raced with the possibilities, already visualising her own name on a centre-spread by-line, with the glorious word 'exclusive' emblazoned across the top. With a story like that she could write her own ticket. Then she stopped herself, a frown creasing her forehead. All very well getting excited, she admonished herself—but how on earth was she to go about getting the story? Slade Keller was notorious for his loathing of the media. In all his years as an actor, he had only granted a handful of interviews—could she really hope to succeed where other much more experienced journalists had failed? Her chin tilted up, the light of battle entering her silvery blue eyes. Damn right she could. Keller might be an uncooperative son of a gun, but he hadn't come across Leigh Daniels before.

With the beginnings of a plan of action already beginning to formulate in her active brain, Leigh quickly paid her bill and left the cafe. Minutes later she was in her much loved, much battered Mini, scouring a map of the island. What was the place name she'd heard the woman say? Loch something or other. Her eyes raced over the map, till with a small whoop of triumph she stabbed her finger right on the spot. Lochranza—that was it. Wasting no more time, she manoeuvred the car out of its space and set off, barely noticing the glorious unspoiled scenery as she rattled along. The best idea at this stage would be to find a place to stay in Lochranza, she decided, and to use it as a base to explore from. Also, if she was actually staying there, it should be easier to strike up some sort of rapport with the locals, and thereby to pick up on the latest gossip. If Keller really was there, it must be the favourite topic right now—but Bill Grant had already warned her that the islanders, though very friendly and hospitable, would be liable to close ranks to protect their own from outsiders. And if Keller's ancestors really had come from Arran, then they would probably consider him as one of their own, no matter how distant the links.

Even though she was thoroughly caught up in her thoughts, her first sight of Lochranza laid out before her as she crested the brow of a hill took her breath away. A motley collection of houses and cottages lay sprawled out around a bay, the weak winter sun sparkling on its calm blue waters. On the shore sat a tiny tumbledown castle. It wasn't a particularly spectacular sight, yet something about the place touched a chord deep within her, as though the village was welcoming her.

She drew to a halt before a small café, climbed out of the car and stood for a moment looking out across the bay with its sprinkling of small boats, breathing in the cool, clear air and feeling a strange sensation of peace. It was—it was as if someone had laid a gentle hand on her brow, she thought with wonder. For long moments she simply stood, drinking in the atmosphere, and when she turned away at last, it was with reluctance.

Remembering her success in the first café, she decided to give the little Lochranza coffee-shop a try, but found to her frustration that it was empty. No chance of eavesdropping on another fruitful conversation here.

'On holiday, are you, miss?' A tall, burly man with a bushy ginger beard and a few strands of reddish hair straggling across a mostly bald head set a tray of coffee and biscuits before her.

'Not exactly,' she demurred, reluctant to commit herself to anything at this stage. 'More of a refresher really. I don't suppose you get many holidaymakers at this time of the year.' She looked up at him guilelessly, praying the query sounded suitably off the cuff.

He shrugged. 'Oh, we get a few. Some people prefer to come here off-season to get the place to themselves.'

'That would be people who already know the island, I imagine.' Leigh took a sip of her coffee, wondering if she was really as transparent as she suddenly felt. Honest and open by nature, it went against the grain to be this devious, but she swallowed hard on the uncomfortable feelings it aroused in her.

'Not always.' The man eyed Leigh curiously. 'You obviously don't know Arran too well yourself.'

She grinned. 'True. But I intend to get to know it a lot better. It's a beautiful place—and so mild! I expected it to be very much colder.'

'Oh, we have our stormy weather.' He seemed to relax. 'But we are generally quite fortunate. You see, the Gulf Stream runs past the island, so we do tend to get milder weather. Haven't you spotted any of our palm-trees yet?'

Leigh chuckled, convinced he was winding her up. 'Palm-trees? You are kidding, surely?'

He shook his head. 'Not at all. People are always surprised by them, particularly our American visitors. They seem to think we've planted artificial ones.'

Leigh laughed along with him, enjoying the way his eyes all but disappeared into his cheeks. 'Are there any on the island at the moment? American tourists that is, not palm-trees.'

It was a gamble to ask such a direct question, but he didn't seem put out by it. 'There are a few—the more discerning ones shall we say, who like to get off the beaten track.'

Leigh waited, but he obviously wasn't about to volunteer any more, and short of asking outright about Slade Keller, she couldn't think of another way to elicit more information. It was frustrating, but instinct warned her not to push too hard. If Keller discovered a journalist was on his tail, he would probably up and vanish.

She was aware of a definite feeling of dissatisfaction as she handed over money to pay her bill, then walked to the counter to collect her change. A good half-hour wasted, and no further forward—and she still had to find a place to stay for the night. A display of accommodation adverts pinned to a noticeboard caught her eye and she idly glanced at it. Several hotels and guest houses were listed, and she was about to reach for her notebook to jot down their names when the words printed on a white postcard near the bottom of the display leapt out at her. 'Want to get right away from it all?' the card questioned. 'Tired of hotel timetables? Then why not consider a holiday cottage?

Take your ease and take your time in one of our cosy homes-from-home.'

'That could be just what I'm looking for.' She hadn't realised she had spoken aloud till she spotted the man's quizzical look. 'The holiday cottages,' she explained with a grin. 'I was just beginning to wonder where I could find a place to stay. A cottage could be just the answer.'

To her dismay, he shook his head, looking slightly uncomfortable. 'The cottages aren't generally let out in the winter,' he began. 'That advert should really have been taken off the board.'

'Oh, damn,' she said, crestfallen. 'Are you sure? Perhaps the owner would make an exception for me.' She had a sudden inspiration. 'I'm a writer, you see, and I'd really like somewhere out of the way. A place where I won't be bothered by anyone.' And a place where no one will question my comings and goings, she added silently.

'A writer?' The man looked interested. 'What are you working on?'

Leigh kept her gaze steady with difficulty. It wasn't a lie, she told herself, just a slight alteration of the truth. 'Let's just say I'm looking for inspiration at the moment,' she said at last.

He grinned. 'That's always been my problem.'

'Are you a writer, then?' It was Leigh's turn to be interested. This could possibly be another story for the paper.

He looked sheepish. 'Not really. At least, I haven't had anything published yet. But I keep scribbling away. Hey—have you written anything I'm likely to have read?'

'I don't think so,' she said hastily. 'It's been mostly specialist stuff up to now. But I'm hoping to try my hand at something new—if I can just get the chance to work it through in my own mind first.'

'Well, you've come to the right place for that.' He seemed to have reached a decision. 'And you're right—a cottage would be the perfect solution. No interruptions, no problem with having to get out of your room for the chambermaid, or having to turn up for meals on time.'

'I couldn't have put it better myself,' Leigh smiled, amused at his enthusiasm. 'So now I just have to convince the owner. Where can I find him?'

'Search no further, lady.' His broad grin was all but swallowed up by the bushy ginger beard. 'You're looking at him.'

She fell in love with the cottage at first sight. Set at the end of a long twisting road that was little more than a cart-track, it was so in tune with its surroundings, it looked as if it had grown alongside the trees rather than been built there.

'Little beauty, isn't she?' The café owner, who had by this time introduced himself as Jack Rayner, had insisted on shutting up shop to take her up to the cottage, stopping on the way to collect groceries. 'As you can see, you're pretty much alone here, though it's only a couple of miles back to the village. And you've got a phone of course.'

'It's gorgeous, Jack.' Leigh gazed round her contentedly. 'I couldn't have asked for anything nicer. Are your other cottages up here too?'

'Cottage,' he corrected her. 'I've just got one other. It's over that way, but you can't see it for the trees.' She followed the direction of his pointing finger. 'Anyway, come on in, I'll show you around.'

She followed him into the cottage, chuckling when he was forced to duck to get through the front door.

'I reckon people must have been built smaller in the old days,' he told her with a rueful grin.

'How old is this place?' Leigh looked round her with pleasure, taking in the exposed wooden beams, whitewashed stone walls and the big old fireplace.

'A couple of hundred years.' Jack fell to his knees before the grate to start laying a fire. 'Of course I've had a fair amount done to it. It was more or less a shell when I first bought it.'

'Is the other one like this?' Curiously she crossed the room to investigate an open archway and found herself in a small kitchen, equipped with a gleaming range, washing-machine and tumble-drier. Much as she loved the olde-worlde charm of the place, it was a considerable relief to know she wouldn't have to wash her clothes in the river.

'Similar. Only it's got two bedrooms where this cottage only has one.' He looked up with a grin as she re-entered the living room. 'The bedroom and bathroom are upstairs. Go see for yourself, I think you'll like them.'

'I feel I should be doing something to help,' she began, but he waved her away.

'You'll have plenty of opportunities to earn your Brownie's badge for laying fires,' he said good-humouredly. 'Make the most of having a slave here to do it for you today.'

Upstairs she gave a little exclamation of delight on walking into the bedroom, her eyes drawn immediately to the shining brass bedstead, and the patchwork quilt spread over the king-size double bed. There was no carpet on the floor, just a couple of rag rugs on the smooth varnished wood, and she immediately started wondering where the rags had come from, and who had so lovingly woven them together. On the unvarnished pine dresser sat an arrangement of dried flowers, and little dishes of pot pourri were liberally scattered about the room, filling the air with the soft fragrance of lavender and honeysuckle.

She felt as though she had been catapulted backwards in time, and for a moment almost forgot the real reason for being there, simply revelling in the loveliness of the place.

'You like?' Jack appeared in the doorway and she turned to greet him.

'Oh, I like, I like! It's so gorgeous, Jack, how can you bear to rent it out to strangers?'

He grinned, pleased by her obvious pleasure.

'Let's just say I'm careful about who I rent it out to. I only take people who'll appreciate the cottage, and look after it.'

'Is this a family heirloom?' She fingered the patchwork quilt with its traditional log-cabin design.

'No. I found it in a sale room, covered in dust and just waiting for the moths. Same with the rag rugs.'

They stood in silence for a moment, sharing the moment of wondering how on earth anyone could treat such precious objects with such disregard.

'Anyway,' Jack spoke at last, breaking the spell, 'I must be off now. Have you everything you need?'

Leigh nodded. 'You've been so kind. I do appreciate it.'

'I know you do. Look, I've jotted down my home phone number and the one for the café on a notepad beside the phone. You will call if you need anything, won't you?'

'I will. But you've seen to everything.' She followed him downstairs and saw him to the door, smiling when he engulfed her hand in his own bear-like paw.

'Good luck with the writing, Leigh. I hope this place inspires you.'

'Well, if it doesn't, nothing will. Thanks for entrusting it to me.'

'Let's just say I've got a soft spot for writers.' And with a wink, he clambered into his car and drove off, bouncing along the rutted track.

His last words left Leigh frowning as she went back into the cottage. She hadn't really told him a lie, she assured herself—she *was* a writer, even if not the kind Jack assumed. So why did she feel as though she had just deceived her best friend? The thought was still plaguing her hours later when she finally turned off the light in the living-room and made her way upstairs to bed.

Perhaps because of an uneasy conscience, Leigh didn't sleep well that night and awoke thoroughly out of sorts. Even the sight of the sunshine dappling through the lace curtains on to her bed couldn't raise her spirits, but she threw back the covers and made her way to the bathroom, determined to shake herself out of her bad mood and get started properly on the hunt for Slade Keller. She still had no real idea where to start looking. Lochranza might be a small village, but she could hardly start knocking on doors. He would soon get wind of her presence if she asked too many questions. And anyway, she reminded herself grouchily, she didn't even know for sure that he really was on the island at all. All she had to go on was that half overheard conversation in the café—those women could have been talking about someone else entirely, and she could waste days searching for someone who was, in all probability, thousands of miles away at this very moment, hard at work on yet another blockbuster film. In fact the more she thought about it, the more ridiculous the whole idea of an American superstar being on a tiny Scottish island seemed.

Thoroughly dispirited, she hauled on a pair of faded old jeans, flat-heeled leather boots and a heavy-knit red sweater. Knowing full well her tumbling golden curls were a sure-fire attention grabber, she twisted her hair into two thick braids. The more she could merge into the scenery the better, and in this get-up she looked like one of the hill walkers and ramblers she had spotted at various points on the island the previous day.

Gulping down the cup of coffee that was all she ever had for breakfast, she reached a decision. If, by that evening, she hadn't come up with some concrete evidence that Keller really was on the island, then she would completely drop the search and get on with something else. After all, she only had a fortnight on Arran, and that didn't allow any time for wild-goose chases. Also, if she came up with nothing, she would seek out Jack and tell him the truth—that she wasn't really a writer at all, but a journalist. Maybe he would be angry enough to throw her out of the cottage, but that was a risk she would just have to take.

Six hours later she swore she would drown if she tried to drink another cup of coffee, and she was feeling positively jittery from a surfeit of the stuff. She must have been in just about every café on the island, she thought wearily, as she headed back along the cart-track to the cottage. If anyone had been following her progress, they would definitely have concluded she was a caffeine addict—or else some kind of a nut. And all for precisely nothing. Oh, people had been friendly enough—a few had even stopped to ask if she was on holiday. But when she had tried to steer the conversation round to more interesting topics, she had been met with blank looks and bemused smiles. No, the more she thought about it, the more pie-eyed the whole notion became. What on earth would someone like Slade Keller be doing in a place like this, beautiful though it undoubtedly was? He probably spent his vacations in the Bahamas, or in some fancy ski-resort. And what did she have to show after a day and a half of searching? Absolutely zilch. The thought of phoning Bill Grant, the newspaper editor, with that piece of information wasn't a cheering one either. Some hot-shot reporter she was turning out to be! Worse still, she had to face seeing Jack and telling him the truth, and that depressed her still more. She could already visualise the disappointment in those friendly, honest brown eyes.

Feeling utterly down in the dumps, she parked the Mini and stood for a moment gazing out over the untroubled view. As unhappy as she was, the peaceful hills and valleys still managed to have a mellowing effect and she breathed deeply of the sweet fresh air, wishing she could empty her mind as easily as emptying her lungs. Strangely unwilling to go indoors, she collected her duffel jacket, scarf and gloves from the car and set off along a path she had spotted the previous evening. It wound its way behind the cottage, through a copse of trees and downwards over ever rockier ground, bringing her out eventually at a small, secluded cove.

There wasn't another soul in sight as she trudged along the pebble-strewn shore, moodily hunching her shoulders in the warm jacket, and kicking up the sand. At the far end of the cove she sat down, leaning against a soft tussock of grass. As she gazed out over the waves she yawned, still weary from the previous night's sleeplessness. Minutes later she was asleep, her head nestled on her folded arms on the grass, quite oblivious of the chill of the air.

She hadn't moved a muscle when the stranger found her there, and she slept on unknowing as he stood before her, a faintly quizzical frown on his face. After a moment, he shrugged his shoulders and sat down at her side, his eyes lazily taking their fill of the long, coltish legs sprawled out on the sand, clearly outlined in their tight blue denim covering. It was impossible to guess her age—with those blonde pigtails she could easily be a schoolgirl, and that heavy jacket ruined his chances of judging her figure. Still, she made a pretty picture lying there, dead to the world. Seemed a shame to disturb her—and she would probably get the fright of her life to see some great hulking stranger sprawled out next to her. But it would soon be growing dark, and he couldn't just leave her there all alone.

He cleared his throat a couple of times, watching closely as she stirred, ready to reassure her that he meant no harm. But when she opened her eyes and looked straight up at him, she smiled the sweetest smile he had ever seen, and for a second the breath just stopped in this throat.

'Hello,' she said sleepily, blinking her silvery eyes. 'I wondered when you'd get here.'

Even with his well known lion's mane of sandy-gold hair dyed dark brown and a droopy Mexican-style moustache hiding that famous sexy lop-sided grin, she would have known him anywhere. All the disguises in the world couldn't hide those glorious tawny eyes, and in any case, the powerful set of his shoulders was an instant give-away. Perhaps she might have passed him by on the street unknowing, but having him this close left no room for doubt.

She suddenly realised she had been lying there grinning up at him like a lovesick calf and pulled herself up into a sitting position, convinced she was blushing scarlet. Well, how could anyone react otherwise on meeting someone as famous?

'Hello yourself, little lady.' The familiar drawl sent a fresh rush of blood to her cheeks and just for a moment she wondered if she was still dreaming. 'Have you been expecting me?'

'Expecting you?' She frowned, not understanding. 'No, of course not. I don't even know who you are.'

He grinned lazily, his eyes openly amused. 'No reason why you should. I just wondered, on account of what you said when you first woke up.'

She looked up at him quizzically, then recalled her own words. Lord above, why had she said such an incredibly stupid thing? She would have been as well saying 'Well, hi there, Slade, how about an interview?' and be done with it.

'I don't know what I meant,' she said at last, nervously picking bits of grass off one thick braid. 'I must still have been dreaming.'

'I reckoned I was dreaming when I first spotted you from back there,' he nodded back towards the beach path. 'You looked like a mermaid lying here.'

'A mermaid?' She chuckled delightedly at the idea.

'Yeah. But then I saw those long legs of yours and realised my mistake.' He let his eyes travel slowly from her leather boots right up to her face. 'Can't say it came as a disappointment, though.'

The look in his lion eyes made her heart stand still for the briefest of seconds, then she mentally shook herself. She had seen that look a dozen times before, bestowed on the various leading ladies he had shared the screen with. It had never failed to get them into bed, and it was a fair bet it had been just as successful in real life. But even without the added lure of his fame, this man was one powerfully attractive animal. Even as the thoughts ran through her mind, she found herself leaning towards him, irresistibly drawn, her lips parted in unconscious invitation. Shaken by the depth of her own response, she abruptly pulled back, hugely irritated by his knowing grin.

'Thanks for waking me,' she said tersely. 'I don't know what came over me to fall asleep here.'

'It's got something to do with the atmosphere of the place.' He leaned back, bracing both hands behind his head. 'One of the islanders warned me about it when I first got here. Takes newcomers by surprise, he said, they keep falling asleep until they get accustomed to the air. Seems it's heavier or something.'

She couldn't help but laugh at his vague explanation. 'Sounds like the old folk-tales when people found themselves under the enchantment of fairies,' she said.

'Could be. That's what they call this place you know—the enchanted isle.'

Again she was caught in the spell of his eyes, held still by his gaze as though something was passing between them that neither could put into words. At last she swallowed hard, dragging her eyes from his.

'Are you on holiday?' Even to her own ears, her voice sounded strained.

'Yes.' The answer was abrupt, and she glanced back at him, surprised. The softness had left his eyes now and there was a tension about the set of his shoulders that hadn't been there before. Damn, she would have to tread carefully if he was going to be this touchy.

'Why Arran?' She pretended not to notice his wariness. After all, it was just the sort of question she would have innocently asked any holiday-maker. She was aware of his careful scrutiny of her face before he answered.

'Why not?'

She grinned. 'Don't bite my head off. I only asked.'

He seemed to relax. 'Sorry. I just don't much like talking about myself.'

'Ah, the strong, silent type.' She resorted to banter though her heart was sinking rapidly. How could she hope to interview someone who wouldn't answer even the simplest of questions? 'My mother warned me about men like you.'

'And I bet she wouldn't be too happy if she knew you were sitting with one of them in a tiny little secluded cove with not another soul in sight.'

It was her turn to be wary. Uneasily she looked about her, realising for the first time just how alone she really was. With his very obvious superiority of strength, she wouldn't stand a cat's chance if he should try anything. He must have spotted the flicker of apprehension in her eyes, for he casually leaned forward to tug one of her braids. 'Don't panic, Goldie,' he said softly. 'I'm not about to pounce on you.' He grinned, his teeth gleaming white and even beneath the moustache. 'After all, we haven't even introduced ourselves yet.'

She let out a long breath. 'I'm Leigh Daniels.' She held out one hand and he took it, his eyes glinting with amusement.

'And I'm Ross Stuart.'

'Really?' She couldn't mask her surprise. 'Doesn't sound very American to me.'

'Scratch an American and you'll find another heritage not too far below.' He was still holding her hand and she felt the warmth of the contact spreading right through her skin. 'Maybe Polish, Irish, Italian, you name it. They all had their good reasons for wanting a new life, and they saw America as the great gateway to freedom. In my case, as you'll gather from the name, my folks came from Scotland.'

'And what took them to America?'

'Guess you could say that's what I'm here to find out.' His lips tightened as soon as he had spoken and it was obvious he regretted letting even that slight piece of information slip. But Leigh deliberately kept her expression impassive and after a second he grinned. 'Come on, mermaid. It's beginning to get dark. We'll never be able to find our way back if we don't leave now.'

He let go of her hand and she felt a second's loss, but it was short-lived as he scrambled to his feet and held out his hand to help her up. This time he held on, tucking her hand companionably into the pocket of his well-worn leather flying jacket as they made their way back along the shore.

'You staying nearby?' he asked.

'In a tiny cottage just up the hill.'

He glanced down at her sharply. 'One of Jack Rayner's?'

She nodded, dismayed by the sudden frown darkening his features. 'Is something wrong with that?'

'I guess not. Except that he assured me he wouldn't let the place to anyone while I was here.' He caught her puzzled expression and smiled, squeezing her fingers gently. 'I've got his other cottage,' he explained. 'It's just a hundred yards or so from your place, but you wouldn't be able to see it for the trees.'

'Jack did tell me about it,' she admitted, 'but he didn't say anything about you.'

'He wouldn't. He knows I like privacy. That's why he promised I wouldn't have a neighbour.'

'I had to work hard at persuading him to let me have the cottage,' Leigh began, anxious to save Jack from any trouble.

'And the poor guy just couldn't resist those eyes, I bet,' he interrupted. 'Can't say I blame him.' He stood slightly to one side to let her go first at a place where the path narrowed, then changed his mind and pulled her round to face him, his free hand cupping her chin. 'I reckon you could persuade just about anybody to do anything you wanted,' he said softly. 'You may not be a mermaid, but there's something of the enchantress about you all the same. Especially in those eyes—they could weave a spell about a man he'd never want to be free of.'

If there was any magic around them, it was all to be found in his hypnotic voice, she thought dazedly, unable to move as he slowly traced a finger over her mouth, letting it rest on the soft fullness of her lower lip. The simple touch all but knocked the knees from under her and she could only gaze at him, longing with an almost overwhelming intensity to feel his lips against her own. The whole world seemed to go into slow motion as he bent over her, his face blocking out the sky, and a pent-up breath escaped her when his mouth grazed her throat. The tiny sound seemed to trigger something in him and he brought both hands up to bury themselves in her hair, pulling her roughly round to feast on her mouth. There was nothing tentative about his kiss, nothing to suggest that the two people clinging together had been strangers until less than an hour before. Leigh felt caught up in the storm of something primitive and previously unknown—yet as instantly familiar to her as her own skin.

She was being held by a man she had never met before, was drowning in the touch of someone who hadn't even told her his real name, swept away by a sudden desperate need that grew only more intense as his tongue slid freely into her mouth. And yet it all seemed so very right and natural—as though she had been waiting all her life for this moment—for this Ross Stuart to come along. Only he wasn't just Ross Stuart. This man was also—primarily—Slade Keller, and she was on the verge of being carried away by some outrageous fantasy, created by a man whose very livelihood centred on his ability to weave fantasies on the silver screen.

The realisation sliced into her like sharp steel and she wrenched herself out of his embrace, staring at him wildly, her breasts heaving as though she had just run a race.

'What's wrong?' He took a step towards her, but she backed away, holding up her hands to ward him off.

'This is crazy,' she gasped. 'We don't even know each other.'

'Try telling that to our bodies,' he bit out. 'They seem to know each other pretty well.'

'That's just moonlight madness or something very like it,' she rationalised, trying to convince herself as much as him.

'Fancy that.' His sense of humour was slowly returning as his heartbeat got back to something like its normal rate. 'And it ain't even moonlight.'

'Please, Ross,' she held out one hand beseechingly, then snatched it back, afraid that the slightest touch would unleash the storm all over again.

'Please, Ross what?' He eyed her speculatively. 'Please, Ross, don't pay any attention to my maidenly protests because I don't mean a word of them? Or perhaps, please, Ross, why don't you take me back to your cottage right now and let's finish what we started?' His eyes glittered strangely. 'Or are you really hypocrite enough to try pretending you weren't fully involved there? Don't bother, lady—I felt you trembling. And it wasn't from the cold.'

She managed to summon up a tremulous smile. 'Maybe not. But I am cold now, Ross.'

The appeal worked. He nodded slowly and grinned, obviously well aware of her ploy. 'OK,

Leigh Daniels, you win. Let's get out of this non-existent moonlight before the madness catches up with us again. Come on, I'll walk you back to your cottage.'

'You don't have to do that.'

He waved away her protest. 'Calm down. I'm not about to storm your front door and carry you off to your bedroom.' His eyes crinkled in amusement. 'I'll wait till you invite me there.'

Unable to cope with his teasing, she turned on her heel and started back along the path, her mind whirling with all that had happened. In the space of a couple of hours she had found the man she had been looking for—only to discover he was masquerading as someone entirely different. More startling still, she had been held in his arms, had been all but carried away by a passion she hadn't even known existed within her. And now he was just a couple of paces behind her. If she stopped walking right now and turned round she could be in his arms all over again, crushed against that powerful body, tasting the incredible sweetness of his kisses. Only stubborn willpower kept her walking.

At the cottage he surprised her again. She had been steeling herself to fight off another physical onslaught, but he simply bent to brush his lips against hers in a kiss as soft as the touch of a butterfly's wing. In its own way it was as devastating to her self-control as those earlier searing caresses and she had to clench her fists to stop her hands clutching him.

'Good night, moonlight lady,' he whispered softly, his eyes telling her he knew exactly how she was feeling. 'Sleep well in that big, lonely old bed.'

CHAPTER FOUR

No matter what she did to distract her mind that evening, she couldn't drag her thoughts away from what had happened that afternoon. And knowing that he—Ross Stuart, or Slade Keller, or whatever he chose to call himself—was just a matter of yards away made her as edgy and restless as a cat.

'I just hope you're feeling equally uncomfortable,' she muttered irritably, flinging herself into the soft comfort of the big old sofa and picking up the book she had already discarded ten minutes before. When she realised she had read the same sentence four times over without taking in a single word, she slammed the book down on to the coffee-table and reached over to switch on the small black and white television set supplied with the cottage. It offered a choice of a game show, a historical drama and a soap opera she usually loved, but tonight just couldn't settle to.

Sighing heavily, she pulled a notebook from her handbag. If he was going to be on her mind anyway, she might as well make the most of it and jot down a few notes about the man. Not that she was likely to forget anything he had said so far—particularly since he had volunteered so little about himself—but it would make her feel better to have a few notes, at least give her the pretence of having something to go on.

Five minutes later she laid down the notebook, having written down all she could think of. It didn't amount to much, certainly not enough to base an article on. Still, at least she now knew he really was on the island, and fate had led him right to her. Now it was up to her to do the rest—but somehow she would have to make sure she never again allowed her senses to overpower her good sense. Only that might not be too easy—he might be an enigma, and a prickly customer to boot, but he was also stunningly gorgeous. And her own willpower was in woefully short supply where he was concerned.

It was a strange thing, she thought broodily, gazing into the flickering flames of the fire she had laboriously built earlier—at twenty-three she had had her fair share of male admirers—possibly even more than her fair share if she were to be honest, since blonde hair seemed to have a magnetism all of its own. If she were to grade them on a scale of one to ten, some would even equal the top marks she had automatically given Ross. Yet not one had managed to stir her the way he had. She had enjoyed their kisses, had even had a few delicious shivers in their arms. But she had never found it difficult to draw the line, or gently to put a stop to proceedings if they tried to go too far. Not that she had any great hang-up about remaining a virgin—as far as she was concerned, making love was a right and vital part of a loving relationship. But she had always been determined to wait until she was involved in something really special—and to cross that final barrier only when her instincts told her it was right. Those instincts had served her well until today—when Ross Stuart barnstormed into her life and threatened to sweep away all her best intentions in one fell swoop.

She had to stop thinking of him as Ross Stuart, she told herself savagely—as Slade Keller he was a famous film star, a quarry to be pinned down on paper, but not a real person. As Ross, he was all too real—a living, breathing man with a body hewn from mountain rock and kisses more potent than mead wine.

If a restless conscience had disturbed her sleep the previous night, this time a restless body was to blame. She tossed and turned, thumping the pillows into countless different shapes in a vain bid to find a comfortable position. And when she did lapse into a fitful doze, it was only to find Ross invading her dreams as well. By morning she was hollow-eyed, with faint violet shadows giving the only touch of colour to her fair skin.

She had a bath and washed her hair, hoping that would bring her to life, then wandered down to the kitchen to make coffee, belting a robe about her still damp body, and absent-mindedly rubbing a towel through her wet hair. As the kettle boiled she glanced through her meagre collection of cosmetics, wondering if she could do anything to make herself look less like the spectre at the feast.

'Hey, don't go using any of that goop on your pretty face!'

She hadn't heard the door open and the unexpected voice made her drop the make-up bag on the floor, its contents scattering across the carpet.

'Now look what you made me do,' she said crossly, trying to ignore the sudden leap her heart had made at the sight of Ross, his broad frame filling the doorway.

'You sure must have a guilty conscience to jump like that.' He crossed the floor in a couple of strides and dropped to his knees to start collecting the fallen items. 'Come on then, don't just stand there looking beautiful—get down here and give me a hand.'

'I don't have a guilty conscience,' she said sulkily, nevertheless doing as she was told and kneeling at his side. 'You just surprised me, that's all.' She crawled away to retrieve a tube of mascara, unaware that he was thoroughly enjoying the view of her pert backside swaying across the floor.

'What are you doing here anyway?' She found her sole lipstick beneath the table and began to back out, still on her knees, only to find herself up against an immovable obstacle.

'I just popped by to say good morning, and to see if you still look as lovely when there isn't any sun as you did when there wasn't any moon.'

She turned sharply to give him a stinging retort, only to find his face a few inches from her own.

'Tell me,' he said softly, 'what would happen if I were to pull this?'

She followed the direction of his eyes downwards and realised he was holding one end of the loosely tied robe belt. Knowing exactly what would happen if he pulled it, she swallowed hard. Now was not the moment to issue challenges.

'I'd rather you didn't,' she said primly.

He grinned, holding his hand up and beginning to draw it back. But just as she was about to lunge forward to stop him, he dropped the belt, letting it fall harmlessly into her lap.

'Perhaps you're right,' he murmured, and his warm breath wafted across her cheek. 'It's always better to let anticipation grow. Makes the end result that much more satisfying. Anyway...' he traced his index finger down into the vee of the robe, 'it's nice to let imagination run riot. For a little while.'

To her consternation the finger lying innocently enough in the valley between her breasts was enough to make her nipples stiffen, and she glanced down, aghast to see the material of the robe wasn't thick enough to cover the tell-tale sign. When she raised her eyes, Ross was grinning broadly.

'I'm happy to see you too, sweetheart.'

'If you'd be good enough to excuse me, I'll go and put some clothes on.' It was a little difficult to muster any kind of dignity under the circumstances, but she did her best.

'Guess you'd better, if we're going out for the day,' he said easily. 'But don't you think you'd better dry your hair first?' He got to his feet and grabbed the towel Leigh had dropped on to the table, and started rubbing her hair, pulling her back effortlessly when she tried to dodge him. 'What colour do you call hair like this, anyway?'

'Blonde. What do you mean, we're going out for the day?'

'No, it's not blonde.' He held a lock of her hair in his fingers, examining it carefully. 'You heard what I said. You got some other plans maybe?'

'No, but that's hardly the point. Why isn't it blonde?'

'Because blonde is a cold colour—there's no life in it. Your hair's like rippling honey. Why isn't it the point? Have I offended your delicate female pride by taking things for granted here? I'm just jumping over a few of the crazy hurdles people set up for each other when they first meet.'

'What's wrong with hurdles? They let people get to know each other before...'

'Before?' He stopped towelling her hair and grinned down at her triumphantly. 'Before they do what they wanted to do in the first place anyway and leap into bed together? What's to know? I learned all I needed to know about you yesterday.'

'Oh, really?' She shot him as disdainful a look as she could manage with wet tangles of hair dangling about her face. 'Which was what exactly?'

He slid the towel down round her neck and used both ends to pull her closer. 'That you're beautiful and sexy, that you kiss like an angel and set my blood on fire, and that you're going to have a hard time keeping me at arm's length.'

His closeness was making her dizzy, and just keeping her breathing steady was a hard enough task on its own.

'If that's a roundabout way of telling me your intentions are less than strictly honourable, I feel I should warn you I grew up with two brothers—I can pack a hefty punch if I need to.'

He smiled. 'I'm glad to hear it. But what happens if it's yourself you're having to fight against?'

'I don't know what you mean,' she said stiffly, lying through her teeth.

'Don't you?' His eyebrows quirked knowingly. 'Listen, honey, I've never forced a woman to do anything she didn't want to do, and I'm not about to start now. But I felt the way you responded to me last night, and I can see the look in your eyes right now—it's as soft and welcoming as any man could ever hope to see in his woman.'

She blinked, horrified that he could read her so easily. But when she started to speak, he hushed her, laying two fingers gently on her mouth.

'Don't be afraid, mermaid. It's a good feeling—an honest feeling. Just because it's come on us both this fast doesn't mean it's any less real. But don't worry—I'll wait for you to give the signal. I won't rush you.'

'What makes you so sure I'll give any kind of signal?' She set her lips in an obstinate line and he chuckled.

'Lady, you've been sending out signals like rockets ever since I first saw you, even if you're not aware of it. Just be grateful I'm gentleman enough to give you a little time before following through.' He put his hands on her shoulders and gently propelled her round to face the stairs. 'Now go get some clothes on, and wear something warm. We've got some serious exploring to do today.' He swatted her playfully on the backside, grinning widely at the outraged expression she threw back over her shoulder. 'Sorry, honey, couldn't resist. Anyway, a guy's got to keep in practice.'

Which was probably exactly what he was trying to do with her, Leigh thought angrily, as she entered the bedroom and started hunting for something to wear. He must be so accustomed to females going all weak-kneed at the sight of him—they would do even if he was an unknown street sweeper instead of an international star. There was just something so incredibly charismatic about him—it had hit her with all the subtlety of a steamroller. In the safety of the bedroom with a closed door and a length of staircase separating them, it was easy to be rational—but it seemed he only had to touch her and her bodily chemistry went haywire. If she had any sense she would put a stop to all this right now, before it got completely out of hand. There was no future in it—he probably had a dozen eager starlets waiting for him back in the States—maybe even a serious relationship. Lord, but the thought hurt. She could just see him with a stunningly beautiful woman wrapped around him, and it stabbed her to the heart. That was just so crazy—she had known him for less than twenty-four hours for goodness' sake! It must be because of all the films she had seen him in, she told herself—she had gazed with wistful hunger on that larger-than-life face on the screen often enough in the past. But the man in the flesh was a hundred times more desirable than that dream figure.

Well, the choice was straightforward enough. She could go back downstairs, make some kind of excuse and get rid of him right now, before any real damage was done. Then she could get on with tracking down a few stories, and make sure she stayed well out of his way from then on in. But to do so would be to give up the best chance she was ever likely to get of a real-life star scoop. At this stage she would have a hard time mustering more than a couple of paragraphs, and Bill Grant would be justifiably furious if she let such a big fish out of the net without even making a sporting attempt at landing him. At the thought of her editor, Leigh frowned. He must be wondering why he hadn't heard from her, but she didn't want to tip him off about Slade Keller too soon. Somehow or other she would have to come up with another story somewhere along the way, just to keep him sweet. As for Ross, or rather Slade, she would simply have to batten down the hatches on her clamouring feelings, win his confidence and his friendship, then choose just the right moment to tell him the truth. By that time she reasoned, he would surely trust her enough to give her an interview.

She scowled at her reflection in the mirror. It all sounded so great in theory—in practice it would probably be akin to roller-skating backwards up Goatfell.

'Are you ready up there?' The drawling voice carried easily up the stairs. 'I'll give you exactly thirty seconds, then I'm coming up there to get you.'

The threat jolted her into action and she grabbed a warm jacket to go over the jeans and sweatshirt she had hauled on a few minutes earlier. No way was she about to let him follow her up here—any room that held not only Ross Stuart but also a big inviting bed could only lead to trouble.

'Where are we going anyway?' She reached the foot of the stairs just as he was about to start ascending.

'I told you. We're going exploring.' His eyes roamed over her figure. 'Nice choice of outfit. But I hope those blue jeans aren't too tight.'

'Too tight for what?' She shot him a suspicious look. 'Just what have you got in mind?'

'I thought we could hire ourselves a couple of push-bikes from the village.'

'Push-bikes?' Her voice rose an octave.

'That's what I said.'

'What's wrong with doing our exploring by car?' she said weakly.

He shook his head. 'Way too fast. You miss too much in a car. This way we can stop every couple of minutes if we feel like it—travel down cart-tracks a car couldn't cope with, smell the good clean air—just enjoy the land properly.' He eyed her challengingly. 'What's wrong, Goldie? Can't you cope with a bike?'

She stuck her chin out resolutely. 'Of course I can. I used to be the best cyclist in school. And they do say you never forget how.'

It was the first of their days together. And looking back with hindsight from five years on, Leigh wondered if it hadn't been in some ways the best of all. On that glorious late winter day, she had had it all—beautiful unspoilt scenery, quiet open roads, the sounds of bird-song in the air, Ross at her side, and an inner peace and contentment she had rarely experienced since. It was a day of light-heartedness and laughter, of shared groans whenever yet another hill appeared on the horizon, of mutual encouragement whenever the going got tough.

Leigh did her best to hang on to the slight grouchiness she had felt earlier that morning, seeing it as at least a slight protection against her own wayward responses, but Ross refused to take her seriously, simply laughing away her curtness until she couldn't keep it up any longer and threw caution to the four winds, teasing him back just as mercilessly. On that day she almost forgot they were each masquerading under false pretences—they were simply Leigh and Ross, two people enjoying each other's company with no hidden secrets to cloud the sun.

They stopped in the early afternoon to picnic on a river bank, sharing bread, cheese and wine from his saddlebag, taking turns to drink from the same bottle and making a long series of toasts, each one sillier than the one before. Later they lay back on the grass to ease their tired muscles and Ross opened up to her a little, telling her tales of his childhood in Wyoming. He had grown up on a ranch, he told her, surrounded by animals and open country, reared on tales of Scotland told by the grandparents who had never forgotten the old country, even though they had left it as newly-weds. He said he'd grown to love the land of his ancestors, even though he had never seen it—and he'd sworn he would go there one day, especially to the tiny island of Arran, where his grandparents had first met and fallen in love.

'They told me it was called the enchanted isle,' he said, his eyes soft with memories of the old folk long gone. 'I thought it was just their nostalgia, till I found the place for myself.'

'Why did they leave?' She was encouraged by his apparent willingness to talk.

'Because there were greater opportunities to be had in America,' he explained. 'And they were right to leave when they did. My grandfather built a spread in Wyoming that was second to none. He could never have had anything like it back here. But he never forgot the place—and he never stopped loving it.'

Then he had turned the conversation to her childhood, and the shadows grew long as she told him about her father, the village teacher, and the old schoolhouse she and her brothers had grown up in.

'We always had a collection of strays around the place,' she said, chuckling softly. 'My dad used to say he'd pack his bags and leave if he came home to find another lame dog or homeless kitten. Then he'd bring home a bird with a broken wing and spend hours trying to make it better. My mum said he was the biggest kid of us all.'

'They sound like nice people.' Ross idly plucked a stem of grass and began chewing on it.

'They are. I was lucky to be born into such a terrific family.'

Somehow they managed to keep clear of any awkward questions—deliberately so on Leigh's part as she didn't want to trigger him to suspicion. It was too early in the game to confess she was a reporter—and in any case, she was enjoying the easy companionship too much to spoil it.

Rather to her surprise, Ross proved as good as his word, and made no attempt to touch her, except to lace her fingers through his as they talked. She found the contact warming, almost reassuring after the intense heat that had flowed between them the previous day.

That night he left her at the cottage door with no more than a gentle kiss on the forehead, and she had gone to bed in a pleasantly dreamy glow to dream sweet dreams, all filled with the man with the laughing eyes.

Without a word being spoken, he casually monopolised the next few days, simply taking it for granted that she would want to be with him on his jaunts round the island. They explored every nook and cranny of the place by car or on foot, and, on a couple of occasions, on horseback. She noticed he seemed to shy away from too much contact with other people, but said nothing, realising he simply didn't want to run the risk of being recognised. In any case, she had no desire to share him with anyone else—though she tried hard not to think about it, she was convinced their time on the island together could be no more than an idyllic interlude, that he would go back to Hollywood at the end of it all, leaving her with sweet memories and, if she was lucky, an exclusive interview. As the days passed, the interview grew less and less important, but she held on to the thought of it as a kind of security—for if it wasn't the main reason for her being with Ross, just what kind of trauma was she facing on parting from him?

As she had expected, Bill Grant had started to hound her for stories, telephoning first thing in the morning to ask if anything was in the pipeline. Terrified he would pull her off the island if she didn't deliver, she managed to cobble a few bits and pieces together, feature ideas gleaned from her trips round Arran and from conversations with Ross, who proved surprisingly knowledgeable about the place. It wasn't really enough to satisfy the editor, but she managed to fob him off with vague hints about a possible major-league story that needed more time.

Time was the real enemy in those long unhurried days, even though it was never spoken of. Leigh knew from newspaper cuttings that Slade Keller was due to start work on a new film in the summer, and though she knew little of the workings of the film industry, it seemed a fair bet that he would be needed for pre-production planning well before the cameras began to roll. Time wasn't on her side either—she had a job and an impatient editor to return to, and she couldn't keep delaying for ever.

But somehow when she was with Ross, thoughts of the outside world never intruded. It was only in the darkness of night that uneasiness penetrated her sleep, brought her awake with a jolt. And that wasn't the only thing troubling her dreams. Though there had been no repeat of the early scorching kisses, the desire still flowed between them, strong and demanding. It was there every time he touched her accidentally, or put a friendly arm about her shoulders, setting light to her senses. She knew he felt the same way, saw the hunger written clear in his tawny brown eyes. Many, many times as they walked and talked together, chatting easily and inconsequentially, she longed for him to forget his promises and simply sweep her into his arms. But he had said he would wait for her to make the invitation and it seemed, to her growing frustration, that he was a man of his word. She knew perfectly well she only had to speak one word, but something always held her back, something she could only describe as fear. In just a few short days he had already become a central figure in her life—waving goodbye to him at the end of it all would be the hardest thing she had ever done. But if she lay with him, loved him, felt the burning power of his passion and then lost him, it would sear her straight to the soul, leaving a scar that would never heal.

Even in her wildest fantasies she never allowed herself to imagine a future with him. He came from such a different world, it could be another planet. Here on the island, he was simply Ross—a man of simple pleasures and easy laughter. But back in the real world, he was Slade Keller, a fêted, much sought-after film star, a man who could snap his fingers and expect any woman to come running.

Leigh had no illusions about her own looks—she knew she was attractive—but in the glamorous circles he was accustomed to she would be overlooked as easily as a tiny candle flame in the midst of flashing neon lights. Holding herself back from the ultimate step of making love was the only protection she could give herself. But climbing into that big empty bed, knowing he was just a few hundred yards away doing the same thing, became harder and more lonely with every night that passed.

Arriving at Glasgow's Central Station in the early hours of the morning, Leigh felt as washed out as the faint grey flickers of dawn creeping into the sullen sky. She had managed to snatch only a couple of short cat-naps as the train thundered through the night, and even then her dreams had taken her back in time.

She trudged across the platform to the cafeteria, still feeling disorientated, longing for a bath and a warm bed. But her journey wasn't over yet. She still had to take another train to the sailing terminal in the seaside town of Ardrossan, then catch the ferry from there to Arran. It was a journey she hadn't ever expected to make again.

CHAPTER FIVE

LEIGH had avoided going anywhere near the ferry during her days with Ross, seeing it as a symbol of their inevitable parting. Eventually it must carry them both back to the mainland, back to reality and separate lives. But together they explored everywhere else, visiting the old haunts of his grandparents, drinking in sights that could hardly have changed since the old folk stood in the same place.

The day that was to prove a turning point in their relationship started off like any other. Ross appeared at the cottage door just as Leigh was making coffee, and he smiled to see she had automatically set out two cups.

'Expecting company?' His eyes were warm and she felt the inevitable tremor of longing.

'Oh, just a drifter who occasionally pops in to say hello,' she said lightly, handing him a cup.

'Is that a fact? You should be real careful who you open your door to, you know. Is he a nice guy this drifter?'

'I think so.' Their eyes held. 'Anyway, this is the enchanted isle, you told me so yourself. It wouldn't let any harm come to me.' Just a shame it couldn't do anything to protect her heart, she thought distantly, because where this man was concerned, it was as vulnerable as a new-born lamb.

'Ready to see a bit more of the enchanted isle, oh lady who opens her door to hobos?'

'Only if the hobo comes with me.'

His eyes caressed her. 'Reckon you can count on that.'

They parked Leigh's car on a quiet stretch of road and made their way up a fairly steep stretch of hillside. Suddenly Ross stopped in his tracks as the sounds of plaintive whimpering floated to them on the still air.

'It's a dog.' Leigh moved to stand beside him. 'Sounds like he's in trouble.'

Ross lifted one hand to hush her, his head tilted to one side as he tried to decide where the sound was coming from. 'He's over to our right,' he said decisively. 'Come on.'

She scrambled after him, finding it hard to keep up as he pushed his way through undergrowth and clambered over boulders. Then she nearly cannoned straight into him as she emerged, flushed and breathless, from a particularly dense patch of shrubbery.

'Careful,' he cautioned, turning to help her through. 'There's a pretty steep drop right at my feet. The dog was probably chasing rabbits and couldn't stop himself in time. I very nearly took a headlong dive myself.'

Leigh followed his pointing finger downward and spotted the animal, wedged in the branches of a tree that had fallen into a river. Only the dog's front quarters were visible, his back legs beneath the water. When he saw Leigh he barked and tried to wriggle, but it was obvious he was stuck fast.

'Oh, the poor thing! We must help him.'

'Sure we'll help him, Goldie,' he grinned down at her. 'Can you make it down there?'

She nodded. 'You lead the way.'

Together they scrambled down the rocky slope, Leigh making most of the trip on her backside.

'Good thing I'm well padded,' she said ruefully, brushing the earth from the seat of her jeans.

'Not by a centimetre too much. But I think you should let me check for bruises later all the same,' Ross said mischievously, and she sent him a haughty look.

'Keep your mind on the task in hand, Mr Stuart. A very wet dog awaits us.'

The animal whined piteously as they reached the fallen tree, obviously delighted to see them.

'Looks as if he must have been trying to haul himself out of the water and misjudged it.' Ross weighed up the situation calmly. 'Can you crawl out along the trunk and talk to him while I go round the other end to try to free him?'

'Of course. I hope he's not badly hurt.'

He shook his head. 'Just well and truly jammed, by the look of it.' He waded out into the river, cursing loudly at the coldness of the water. Leigh clambered on to the tree trunk and started edging her way forward, gripping with her knees, speaking softly to the dog as she went. She reached the animal just as Ross did, but saw immediately there was little she could do from her side.

'He's trapped underneath the water,' she said, stretching out one hand to stroke the dog's silky head and smiling as he tried to twist round to lick her. 'Looks as if he's glad to see us.'

'Smart fellow. Keep talking to him while I check out the problem. I don't want to frighten him now.'

Leigh murmured soft crooning words of comfort as Ross crouched in the water, his hands gently feeling along the animal's body.

'Can you free him?' she asked anxiously.

'Sure, but he's pretty tightly stuck. Probably just made things worse by trying to wriggle out himself. Crazy pooch! Just watch that mouth of his—he might try to bite if I accidentally hurt him.'

'You wouldn't bite me, would you boy?' Leigh gently pulled the floppy ears.

'Couldn't say I'd blame him if he did.' Ross frowned in concentration as he slowly began to ease the animal free.

'What do you mean?' She shot him a puzzled look.

'I wouldn't mind biting you myself.' Before she could think of a reply, he gave a great shout of triumph, the dog suddenly shot forward and launched itself at Leigh, barking wildly in a frenzy of delight. Taken completely by surprise, she opened her arms, lost her grip on the tree trunk and was knocked clean off balance by the excited animal. The two of them landed with a colossal splash at Ross's feet and he roared with laughter at the sight.

'Don't just stand there, you great lunk,' she spluttered. 'Help me up.'

Still laughing, he reached down, but instead of taking his hand, she grabbed his jacket and gave it a single almighty tug, dodging to the side as he plummeted down beside her. The dog splashed about them, thinking this was all part of the game.

'You little witch! What did you do that for? Now I'm as wet as you are!'

'Exactly,' she said smugly. 'I didn't see why just one of us should have to suffer a wet backside all the way home.'

'Is that a fact? Well, let's just see how you like this, madam mermaid.' He scooped up a great handful of water, sending it cascading over her face and hair. It was the signal for all-out war and within seconds they were cavorting in the water like a pair of schoolchildren, quite oblivious of the cold.

When she tried to scramble to her feet he grabbed her round the middle and hauled her down again, and when he attempted to crawl away to the river-bank, she barged into him and sent him sprawling.

'Lady, you are definitely playing with fire.' His eyes glinted wickedly as she backed away to safety.

'I think you've got your elements a little confused,' she said pertly. 'This wet stuff is water, not fire.'

'But that ain't the fire I'm talking about.' He made a sudden lunge forward and grabbed her by the knees, using her body as a support to pull himself up. The giggle died in her throat as he towered over her, his eyes darkening. Slowly his hands slid down to mould her backside and he lifted her clean out of the river as easily as if she had been made of thistledown. She was beginning to shiver from the cold, but the feel of his hard body pressing against her own brought a new heat all of its own. Completely forgetting all her best resolutions, she slid her arms round his neck, burying her hands in his wet mane of hair, murmuring his name deep in her throat.

'God, Leigh, you don't know how hard it's been,' he groaned. 'Being with you every day and never touching you. If you knew all the things I've been longing to do.' His lips grazed her throat and her heart sang wildly at his impassioned words. 'Tell me you feel the same way,' he murmured huskily. 'I can't wait any longer for you to say the words.'

'I do want you, Ross.' The words were torn from her by a need too deep to suppress any longer. 'But it's too soon.'

'Too soon? Not for us, moonlight lady. If we'd made love there on the beach that very first day it wouldn't have been too soon. Didn't I tell you then that our bodies knew each other?'

'But Ross...'

'No, honey. No matter what words those beautiful lips say, they tell me a very different story when they kiss me.' As if to prove his point he dipped his head to claim her mouth and her arguments took flight, her powers of conscious thought disintegrating with the gentle pressure of his teasing lips. She barely noticed that he was carrying her out of the river until he set her tenderly on the bank.

'I think we should go back to the cottage right now,' he said softly, his eyes gleaming tawny bright. 'Get out of these wet clothes.'

'What about the dog?' She knew full well what he was really saying and only a tiny part of her mind was capable of resisting what had been so inevitable all along.

'He's OK. Look.' She turned her head to see the little animal scampering away up the hillside.

'Shouldn't we make sure he gets home all right?' she said weakly.

'I'll lay bets he knows the countryside better than we do.' There was tender amusement in his eyes as he gently stroked a strand of hair from her face.

'But he still managed to fall down the hill.'

Ross grinned. 'Anyone can make a mistake. Now—shall we go home?'

She swallowed hard, hardly able to meet his knowing eyes. At last she nodded.

'Come on, then.'

Back at the cottage she almost began to wonder if she had been struck down by some sudden and weird illness. Her movements were strangely jerky, her mouth felt dry as a desert, and her co-ordination had vanished on the wind. She dropped her wet jacket on the pathway outside the door, then scattered the contents of her handbag when she bent to pick up the jacket. Ross helped her collect the fallen items, but made no comment. Feeling his gaze upon her, she wondered if she really was as transparent as she suddenly felt—if he could really see straight through to the heart that was beating nineteen to the dozen.

'Go get yourself into a nice hot bath.' He placed the strap of her handbag back on her shoulder. 'You're shivering.'

'What are you going to do?' She licked her dry lips, knowing it wasn't just the damp clothes that were making her shiver.

'I'm going to have a bath too.'

'Back at your own cottage?' His words sent a flood of relief washing over her. For the moment at least, she had been reprieved—even if honesty did force her to admit there was more than a tinge of disappointment there too. 'OK. I'll see you later.'

He tipped an imaginary hat and she made her way to the bathroom, turning the taps full on and adding a generous amount of bubble bath. She stripped off her wet clothes and dumped them in the wicker laundry basket, then slid gratefully into the silken water, closing her eyes as the warmth caressed her limbs. Seconds later her eyes flew open and she gave a strangled yelp as the door was flung open and a barefoot Ross walked calmly in, carrying two glasses of what looked like brandy.

'My God, Ross!' She made a frantic effort to cover herself with her hands, then realised the foaming bubbles were already doing the job for her. All the same, she felt utterly exposed as his eyes ran rakishly over her.

'Relax,' he said easily. 'I thought the brandy could warm our insides while the bathwater takes care of the rest.' He set the glasses down and before her amazed eyes began unbuttoning his shirt.

'Ross!' She sat bolt upright, then realised her mistake and slid quickly back down into the concealing water. 'I thought you said you were going back to your own place.'

'Correction, sweetheart,' he said lazily, pulling the shirt free from his trousers. '*You* said I was going back to my place. I just didn't disagree, that's all.' He dropped the shirt to the floor and she gazed mesmerised at the rippling muscles in his tanned torso. She had always wondered if the width of his shoulders came from extra padding in his clothes—now she could see it was all built in. Her glazed eyes focused in on the thick mat of dark hair on his chest and she wondered vaguely if the hot water was to blame for her sudden attack of light-headedness.

'What are you doing?' she said weakly.

'Guess that should be obvious.' He slid the buckle of his belt free and slowly slid down the zip on his jeans. 'I'm coming in there to keep you company.'

'You're what? You can't! There's no room.' Her cheeks burned as the jeans joined the shirt on the floor, but for the life of her she couldn't drag her eyes away from the glorious sight of his almost naked body.

'Well, let's just put that to the test.' He hooked his thumbs into the waistband of his scarlet boxer shorts and she groaned, wondering if this was all some crazy dream she would soon waken from.

'Move over a bit.'

Too stunned to protest further she slid forward obediently and he climbed in behind her, bracing his knees at either side of her.

'You're right,' he grumbled. 'This bath ain't really big enough for both of us.' He casually slung one leg over the rim of the bath, and she gave an involuntary squeak as his arms closed around her, pulling her hard back against his chest. 'But I reckon we can manage, can't we, Goldie.' The words murmured along her neck and she shivered when his lips homed straight in on a sensitive spot on her shoulder she hadn't even known she possessed. He picked up a bar of soap from a dish at the side of the bath and began rubbing up a lather in his hands.

'Best way I know of to get the circulation going.' His fingers spread the creamy foam over her back, then slid underneath her arms to cup her breasts. She opened her mouth to protest, then slowly closed it again. How could she protest at something that felt so good—so right? He had never touched her this intimately before—come to that, nor had anyone else—yet he seemed to know through sheer instinct what would pleasure her most.

'Turn round so I can do your legs.'

Still suffering from a strange shyness, she tried to turn round and slide back beneath the water, but his legs got in the way. Instinctively she crossed her arms over her breasts, but he lifted them away.

'You're beautiful, moonlight lady,' he said softly. 'My hands have already found that out for themselves. You can't deny my eyes the same pleasure.' Still holding her hands captive, he looked his fill and she felt her nipples harden beneath his gaze.

'You see?' he whispered. 'Your body knows just how to act, even if your crazy mind's trying to mess things up.'

He reached for her foot and began soaping it, glancing up in surprise when she tried to pull back.

'You don't have to do that,' she murmured breathlessly.

'But I want to.' He planted her foot more firmly on his bent knee. 'You've got lovely little toes. Hasn't anyone ever told you that before?' She shook her head, mesmerised by the ripples coursing right through her skin. His massaging fingers crept slowly upward, along the calf, across the knee, along the soft flesh of her inner thigh. Her mouth had stopped working long ago, now it seemed her brain followed suit. Every cell in her body trembled as his hand crept slowly up, up...

'Guess we'll have to finish this bath some other time.' His voice was strangely ragged.

'What?' She dragged up the word through vocal cords grown choked.

'A man can only take so much.' He grinned, but the effort of self-restraint was clear in his eyes. 'And I think I've just reached the limit.' He held out his hand and slowly she stood up with him, moving like a creature in a dream. He wrapped her in a huge fluffy bath towel, gently rubbing her dry, then scooped her into his arms.

'You're still wet,' she murmured.

'Don't worry. I won't rust.' He carried her through to the bedroom and laid her on the bed, then peeled away the towel, his eyes devouring her naked body.

'I've dreamt of seeing you like this,' he said huskily, 'but my dreams haven't done you justice. You're more beautiful than anything I could ever have imagined.'

His soft words took away the last traces of her reserve and she gladly held her arms open to him in willing invitation, gasping aloud to feel for the very first time the exquisite sweetness of his naked body pressed against her own. His fingers stroked her satiny skin and with each featherlight caress it was as though a burning river rippled through her blood, turning her to fire in his arms. The hair on his chest tickled her breasts and she moved restlessly, aching to be closer still.

'Easy, sweetheart,' he groaned. 'I'm on a short fuse here.' He slid downwards to nuzzle her breasts, his tongue circling the swollen brown peaks, and she buried her hands in his thick, curling hair, urging him to be more demanding still, moaning deep in her throat when his mouth closed over one aching peak, the flicking sensation of his velvet tongue sending her senses reeling. His hand stroked the length of her thigh and she trembled wildly when his fingers touched the soft curls at the base of her stomach, then moved unerringly down, dipping into the very heart of her craving. She arched up to meet his hand and he laughed, pulling her closer still.

'I knew it would be like this,' he murmured, and she thrilled to the soft note of triumph in his voice. 'I knew you'd be soft and sweet and ready to burn when I touched you.' He raised himself up on one elbow and she gazed at him through passion-clouded eyes. 'Are you all right, sweetheart? Do you need me to take care of things?'

She was too far gone to voice an answer to his tender question, but managed to shake her head.

For a second he gazed into her mesmerised eyes, feeling the thrust of her breasts against his chest, his hands clasping the narrow curve of her waist. 'You are the loveliest sight I've ever seen, Leigh Daniels,' he whispered, 'with your golden hair spread out on the pillow and your sweet lips so soft and inviting. I could look at you like this for ever, my island enchantress.'

'Love me, Ross.' She was barely aware of having spoken, couldn't tell where the words had come from, only knew the need building up within, too powerful to be denied. She saw the smile curving his lips beneath the luxuriant moustache, felt his knee edge her legs farther apart, and slowly, tantalisingly, he slid himself into her. There was a tiny sensation of pain and she cried out softly, then all was pleasure as she felt the strength of him deep inside, fulfilling her, enslaving her. She began to move with him, her body responding to his through sheer untrained instinct, the pressure building up until she felt the whole world must surely explode with it. From a million miles away she heard his voice, murmuring soft sensuous words, and she felt as though she were flying through space, minute flashes of coloured light bursting behind her closed eyes. The raging torrents carried her to a high, uncharted peak, miles above any mountain ever conquered by man. At last the turbulent tides began to ebb slowly away and she opened her eyes to see his smile.

'Why didn't you tell me?'

'Tell you?' Her mind was still too full of all it had seen to function properly.

'That you were a virgin.' He stroked a strand of hair from her eyes. 'I would have gone much more slowly if I'd known.'

She shook her head, stretching in his arms as languorously as a cat. 'I wouldn't have wanted you to. Oh, Ross, that was so—so incredible!'

He hugged her. 'For me too, honey. But I thought you said you were protected. How come?'

She coloured slightly. 'My doctor put me on the pill a couple of years ago to—well, to regulate me.'

'And yet you've never slept with anyone, even though you'd have been safe to?' His eyes gazed at her steadily. 'Why not?'

She shook her head. It was a question she wasn't ready to answer yet, even to herself. 'I don't know,' she said at last. 'It's just never seemed right before.'

'Well,' he drawled the word out, slowly dipping his head till their noses touched, 'guess all I can say is—three cheers for your doctor,' and her laughter was swallowed up in his kiss.

They barely slept that night, turning again and again to each other's arms, the darkness filled with the soft sounds of lovemaking, or the murmured tones of low, unhurried conversation. In her memory now, the many times when their bodies had entwined mingled into a glorious kaleidoscope. For the rest of their time together she had never slept alone—waking up in the morning became a whole new experience of greeting the new day with a gentle and sleepy passion, going to bed at night a wonderful tangle of limbs. Ross even introduced her to the joys of making love out of doors and they frolicked in the early spring days like two young animals.

But gazing out over the ferry bow towards the hazy outlines of the island just appearing on the horizon, Leigh knew that first night together would always remain indelibly etched in her memory, a picture diamond-cut on glass. On that night she had given not only her body but her soul to the man who had loved her so tenderly. It was a night that had haunted her over the years till she had learned to shut the memories away, for it was impossible to think of them without opening the floodgates to the much more agonising pictures of the day when her world had fallen apart.

She turned away from the bow, a frown creasing her eyebrows. She had deliberately avoided thinking about that day, hadn't been ready to face up to it. But the time was approaching fast, and she knew she couldn't keep the barriers up forever. Having travelled all these miles to get back to the island, she now had only a short distance to go to reach the place where it had all happened, and it was bound to trigger off all those painful, unwanted thoughts.

She wandered absent-mindedly below decks to collect her luggage, barely aware of the other passengers mingling about her, intent on their own business. As the ferry approached the jetty, she joined the line of people queuing to disembark, resolutely swallowing hard on the first faint feelings of panic creeping into her chest, making steady breathing difficult. Just what the hell was she doing here anyway? she wondered helplessly as the doors opened and she was carried along towards the exit with the flow. How could she have let herself be talked into this unbelievably crazy venture—and what did she expect to happen anyway, other than more heartache at the end of it all? That brief, embarrassing episode with Ross—no, with Slade, she reminded herself angrily—in the hotel bedroom had surely been enough to prove there could never be anything between them other than bitterness, yet here she was, voluntarily delivering herself up all over again.

'Mind your step now, miss.' One of the ferry stewards caught her arm as she stumbled at the open doorway. 'Wouldn't want you to take a fall now—it could ruin your holiday.'

She managed to summon up a rueful grin as she thanked him. As if anything could spoil this so-called holiday—it already held all the elements of total self-destruction. Just so long as you don't let yourself get destroyed in the process—the tiny voice came from nowhere, echoing in the back of her mind, and she unconsciously lifted her head in a gesture of defiance. No way, Buster, she murmured angrily under her breath—you knocked the wind clean out of my sails last time and left me sailing solo on an unkind empty sea—but I made it. And I'll make it again, no matter what little tricks you've got in store for me. The words of self-reassurance carried her down the gangway and on to the jetty, arming her against the inevitable pang she felt on first setting foot on the island again.

She walked away from the ferry, turning on to the main road through the village of Brodick, pausing to gaze out over the beautiful blue waters of the bay across to the solid structure of the castle nestled against Goatfell. A tiny sigh escaped her as she stood, letting her eyes drink their fill of the view, aware of an inner gladness that this much at least hadn't changed at all. And all over again she felt that inner sense of peace as though someone had laid a comforting hand on her shoulder. A smile played about her lips—no matter what sort of reception he had in store for her, Arran at least had welcomed her back.

CHAPTER SIX

'It's Leigh, isn't it? Leigh Daniels?'

She whipped round, startled by the sound of her own name, and found herself face to chest with a huge bear of a man. Her eyes travelled swiftly up to his face, and an irrepressible grin creased her eyes as she recognised the familiar features.

'Jack Rayner!' Impulsively she held out both hands, laughing as they were engulfed in his great paws. 'What are you doing here?'

'Well, I could ask you the same thing,' he said mildly. 'After all, I do live here, remember?'

'Of course I remember, you great ox,' she chuckled, relief at finding a friendly face making her quite light-headed. 'How could I ever forget you?'

'Well, you seem to have done your best over the past—how many years is it—five? What brings you back here now?'

She started to answer then stopped, not quite trusting his over-innocent look. 'You know why I'm here, Jack,' she said slowly. 'Don't you?'

He shuffled uncomfortably, not quite meeting her eyes. 'Not exactly. I mean, I knew you were coming—I just don't quite know why.'

Thank heaven for small mercies, she thought distantly. Five years before, Jack had been just about the only other person allowed into the private world Leigh and Ross had carved for themselves. They had occasionally stopped to have coffee at his little restaurant, and once he had cooked them a special dinner, closing the place off to other guests so that they could have it to themselves, utterly entranced by the romance he saw developing between his two tenants. When Ross left, slamming the door on all Leigh's dreams, it had been Jack she had run to, and he had opened his arms to her, offering comfort without asking a single question. She hadn't been able to tell him the truth then, and frankly she felt the words might choke her if she tried to explain now.

'I'm not sure I know myself why I've come back,' she said slowly, focusing on the red-brown thatch of beard obscuring the lower half of his face. 'Maybe you could say the island drew me back.'

He nodded understandingly. 'If that's the case then you were right to come back. The island knows what it's doing.' Then he grinned broadly and flung his arms about her in a crushing bear-hug that all but suffocated her. 'Anyway, who cares? It's great having you back, no matter what the reason is.'

'Jack, is this meeting just a coincidence? Or did you know I was arriving today?' With difficulty she managed to extricate herself enough to draw breath.

He looked a little sheepish. 'I knew you'd probably get here today from what I'd been told. Let's just say I couldn't resist the opportunity to see those pretty blue eyes again. Anyway, I always like to greet my tenants personally.'

'Tenants?' She drew back in his arms, frowning up at him. 'But I never...'

'Booked a cottage? No, I know you didn't. But Ross did—he contacted me a while ago to ask for both cottages to be reserved. When he turned up alone I had a sneaking feeling you wouldn't be far behind.' He took her arm, easily hoisting her suitcase in the other hand, and started walking towards his car.

'A while ago?' Leigh shot him a suspicious look. 'How long exactly?'

'I'm not sure,' he replied vaguely, fumbling in his pocket for the car keys. 'A couple of weeks maybe.'

Leigh felt a wave of anger. So Ross had been so sure she'd simply fall in with his plans, had he? Damn the man and his cocksure arrogance.

'I'm not so sure I really want to stay in the cottage, thanks all the same,' she said stiffly. 'Perhaps I'd be better in a hotel.'

Jack threw her case in the back seat of the car and looked up at her in pained surprise. 'Aw, Leigh, don't disappoint me. I never took you for a coward.'

'A coward?' She all but yelped the words, her voice rising an octave.

'Sure. I know the place holds sad memories for you, even though you never did tell me the full story. But I've got eyes and ears—and a vivid imagination. I've also got a heart of my own, and it knows what it feels like to be broken. It's always best to face up to what scares you, Leigh—take it from one who's been there.'

She subsided into the passenger seat, wondering at the strange look she had spotted in his warm brown eyes. Just what exactly had he been trying to say with those few guarded words? She had always been aware, even in the heady days when Ross had been the centre of all existence, that Jack was fond of her—but had there been more to it than that? Was he, in his own way, facing up to a pain of his own by meeting her again after all those years? Her eyes softened as she slid him an assessing look. If that was true, he was an even finer person than she had given him credit for—for here he was, blithely driving her to meet with her former lover, and all the while keeping his own feelings as close to his heart as ever. She felt the sting of tears behind her eyes—why did love have to be such a savagely arbitrary thing? It flung its arrows wherever it chose, without ever stopping to think of the consequences for its victims.

'The old place hasn't changed much, huh?' She forced her voice to remain steady as she spoke, gazing out over the countryside.

'Thank God,' Jack returned fervently. 'I'd up and leave if it ever did.'

'I didn't think I'd ever come back,' she said softly. 'I didn't think I'd ever be able to face the island again.'

'Didn't you?' He turned his head to look at her with his usual scant regard for safety and she winced as another car only just managed to scrape past on the narrow stretch of road. 'I always believed you'd be back some time. In any case, you can't blame

Arran for what happened between you and Ross—whatever it was.'

'I didn't—I don't,' she said quickly. 'If anything, it was the other way round. I mean, I felt guilty that I'd allowed it all to happen on such a special place—as if the island would somehow blame me.' She gave a sad little smile. 'Sounds crazy, huh?'

He shook his head. 'Not to me. But even if it was all your fault, don't you think you should forgive yourself now? The island surely has.'

They drove in silence for a while, Leigh musing over Jack's words. As they drew closer to Lochranza, she turned to him again, her voice hesitant. 'How much do you really know, Jack?'

'About you and Ross? Not much—but enough. Enough to know you both had secrets you kept from one another—stupid destructive secrets that finally ruined something very special.'

'Did you know his secret?'

He threw her a knowing look. 'That he was really Slade Keller, mega-famous film star? Sure, I knew that. Come to that, so did every other islander.'

His casual words caught her like a blow to the stomach. 'They knew? Then why...'

'Why did they keep quiet? Because they knew he'd come here for privacy—to escape from his own crazy world. They weren't going to intrude on that.'

There was no criticism in his words, no hint of judgement, yet she felt he had laid bare her soul. Those other strangers, those nameless, faceless people, had been prepared to give Slade Keller something which she, at the very start of it all, had set out to plunder—his right to anonymity in a world where he could rarely walk unrecognised. For a second she felt a deep sense of shame, then Jack's warm hand covered her restless fingers.

'You wouldn't have done it, Leigh. At the end of the day, no matter what happened between you, you wouldn't have written the story.'

His words warmed her even as she gazed at him in surprise. 'You knew that too? You knew that I was a reporter?'

"I didn't know then—but I've seen quite a few of your articles since. You're a fine writer, Leigh—you never seem to go in for that gutter stuff.'

'I don't,' she said simply. 'Not ever. But I wonder if I'll ever be able to convince him of that.'

'You'll soon have the chance to find out.' Jack drew slowly to a halt before the little whitewashed cottage she remembered so well, and she took a deep, unsteady breath.

'Won't you come in? Have a coffee or something?' Her words trailed away as she caught the look in his eyes.

'No, honey. This is something you'll have to face for yourself. But you know where I am if the going gets tough—and I won't turn away.' He carried her case to the front door, and planted a swift, brotherly kiss on her cheek. 'He's a lucky swine if he but knew it,' he said tenderly. 'Just make sure he finds it out.' And then he was gone, leaving her alone at the door, gazing after the disappearing car. It took her a few moments to gather enough courage to enter the cottage, but at last she did, steeling herself for the inevitable onslaught of memories. The place looked much the same—perhaps a fresh lick of paint here and there, and the suite had been re-covered, but the atmosphere was unchanged. Moving slowly she carried her case upstairs, passing by the bathroom door without looking in. She would face that particular memory later—first she had to cope with seeing the bedroom. She pushed the door open tentatively, almost expecting to see Ross lying there on the great king-size bed, sprawled over the patchwork quilt as he had been so often, his eyes lazily watching her move about the room, or holding out his arms to draw her back to bed. And the pain was there all right—even though she had been expecting it, she was stunned by the sheer slicing weight of it, cutting through her very bones like a dagger. Face it, she told herself angrily, don't try to hide. The time for hiding has long gone.

She moved slowly to the bed and carefully sat down, tracing one finger over the log cabin design of the quilt. She could easily have sketched it from memory. She kicked off her shoes and lay down in its soft depths, suddenly overcome by a weariness she had been battling ever since stepping on to the ferry. She would have to sleep before she could face seeing him—had to gather as much strength as possible before that ordeal. And there was something else too—before that meeting, she must face up to that last dreaded memory—complete the running film she had allowed to play in her mind. Her eyelashes fluttered down on to her cheek as the images crowded into her mind and she drifted slowly into sleep.

* * *

She had wakened early that morning, turning automatically to look at the man still sleeping at her side. He had told her he was thirty-three—in sleep he looked several years younger and it wasn't hard to visualise the young lad who had grown to manhood on the Wyoming ranch before the lures of Hollywood drew him away. Idly she wondered what his life would have been like if he had stayed on the ranch—and just why had he left anyway? So many things she didn't know about him, yet she felt closer to this man than to anyone else she had ever known. And it wasn't just because of the many times they'd lain in each other's arms—she had grown to cherish his tenderness, his crazy sense of humour that could find fun in the dullest of things, his lively enquiring mind. She had seen flashes of a darker side too, when his eyes would hold shadows he wouldn't explain—but with her he'd only ever been gentle.

Troubled by the way her thoughts were going, she frowned faintly—right from the start she had been afraid to let him get too close, afraid to open up to something that could have no future. But somehow, over the days, she had allowed the barriers to fall without ever consciously realising it. She had all but laid down a red carpet and begged him to cross, so now she had only herself to blame if he was lodged firmly in her heart.

She lay back on the pillow, hearing the soft, rhythmical breathing of the man at her side. She had never intended to let this happen—she'd known from the start she was playing with fire, but she had been so sure she could cope. Now she was having to face up to something she'd been trying to deny ever since this crazy affair first started—that she was falling in love with Ross Stuart. She smiled mirthlessly at her own careful but inaccurate choice of words—there was no longer any question of 'falling'—she had already fallen, hook, line and sinker. The very fact that she was lying beside him proved it, if she needed any proof. She could never have given herself so freely, so easily to any man unless her heart had been fully in control. But could that really be possible in such a short time? She had never really believed in love at first sight—now she wasn't so sure. She'd started losing a grip on all her good sense the very second she opened her eyes on the beach to find herself gazing into smiling tawny eyes. Even if he'd walked away from her then without saying a word, she would never have been able to forget him completely. But having been with him, having laughed and argued and played with him—having lain in his arms and skyrocketed to the stars with him—how in creation's sweet name could she hope to forget him now?

The thought of the article was little more than a crazy joke now. She could never calmly sit down and attempt to commit all she knew of him to paper—could never bring herself to share the man she knew with others. And the time had come to tell him that, even though he had never even known what she had originally had in mind. The thought blocked the breath in her throat—owning up to him would be the hardest thing she had ever done, and she was already afraid of what she would see in his eyes. Would there be disappointment? Contempt? Or would he be understanding and thank her for her honesty? Whatever, she had to go through with it. Realising the depth of her feelings for him, she couldn't do anything else—love this strong demanded honesty, not deceit.

Her decision made, she slipped out of bed, padding quietly on bare feet to the bathroom. A quick shower, then she would make breakfast for them both and serve it to Ross in bed. A soft smile touched her lips at the thought—knowing his appetites, he would doubtless want more than just breakfast in bed, but she had no objection to that. Her hunger for him hadn't diminished one jot in the days since he had first climbed into the bath beside her. Afterwards, she decided, stepping under the warm rush of water, they could go for a walk, and she would tell him everything. But first she would telephone her editor—the paper owed her a couple of weeks' holiday and she intended to claim them right now. Ross still hadn't made any mention of how much longer he could stay, but wild horses wouldn't drag her back to the mainland while he was still on the island. Bill Grant probably wouldn't be delighted at being given such short notice, but for once in her life she would be stubborn, and if necessary remind him of all the extra hours she had gladly put in without ever asking for time off in lieu.

Half an hour later she laid down the telephone with a satisfied smile. Bill had ranted a little, but had given in, after making her promise she would bring back a notebook full of stories at the end of it all.

She went through to the kitchen, humming softly under her breath as the aroma of frying bacon filled the air, flipping the egg over to harden just the way Ross liked it. She was just filling the coffee percolator when he walked in, fully dressed.

'Hi,' she said softly. 'You shouldn't have got up. I was just coming back to bed.'

'Hoping for some more revealing pillow talk?' His harsh, unexpected words cut her like a whiplash. 'Tell me, Leigh, have you been running a tape recorder beneath the bed, or do you simply memorise every word in that conniving little brain of yours?'

Startled she stared back at him, wondering what on earth had happened to turn the tender lover of just a few hours before into this bleak-eyed stranger.

'What's happened?' She took a step towards him, but the look on his face halted her. It was a look of ice-cold fury and it chilled her to the soul. 'Ross, tell me! What's going on?'

'Drop the act, sugar.' She flinched at the undisguised contempt in his voice. 'Ross Stuart just took a hike. But congratulations, you really had him fooled for a little while there. You really managed to make him believe you were turned on by him—that you were maybe even falling a little in love with him.' His lips curled in a sneer. 'But you've been after a much bigger fish, haven't you? How does it go again? "Slade Keller, darling of the screen, yet a real-life enigma. Keeps his private life very much under wraps—even uses disguises when he wants to stay incognito."'

The colour drained from her face as she recognised the words she had scrawled in her notebook on the very first night of meeting him.

'Shall I go on? "Presently calling himself Ross Stuart and fooling the world with dyed hair and a Mexican moustache".' He eyed her bitterly. 'And here comes the unkindest cut of all. Why did you go to such pains to cover up the fact that you've known about me all along?' With a look of disgust, he flung something down on to the kitchen table. It was her Press card. 'Because you're a journalist. One of the God-damn parasites of the world. You people make me sick,' he ground out. 'You'd sell your own grandmothers for a half-decent story.'

'Ross, that's not true!'

'The name's Slade, honey, so let's not play any more silly games. And don't try perjuring your soul—you haven't just sold me out, you've prostituted yourself to do it. What did you think—that I'd spill my guts for you just because I'd had the use of your body a few times? I guess I should be flattered—you obviously saw me as a real prize catch if you were willing to give up your precious twenty-three-year-old virginity to me. Or was it simply that you'd never met anyone famous enough to squander it on before?'

She stood before him, bowed down by the weight of her misery, unable to say a single word in her own defence. He had taken the facts, twisted them beyond belief, till she shuddered at the warped view he presented of her—but in essence he was right—

she had wanted him first and foremost for the story she thought she could write. In his anger he would never believe that she had long since ditched any intention of writing the story.

'Where did you find the Press card?' She pushed the words through dry lips.

'In your bag, along with your oh-so-informative notebook.' His eyes narrowed dangerously. 'I suppose you find it reprehensible that I should rummage in your possessions—well, it ain't nearly as bad as rummaging in someone's life, lady.'

'Ross, please—I wish you'd let me at least try to explain.' Unthinkingly she held out one hand to him in a beseeching gesture, but he ignored it.

'For the last time, the name is Slade,' he bit out. 'As far as you're concerned Ross Stuart is dead and gone for ever. But I don't figure that should bother you too much, since it was never him you wanted anyway.'

She longed to tell him he had got it all wrong—that she had wanted only the man who had held her in his arms, that she had already wished a thousand times he really was Ross Stuart, a man without a secret life. She longed to tell him she had fallen in love with that man, but the words stuck in her throat. He would only throw them back in her face—he was too angry and embittered to listen to a word she said.

'Well, I wish you luck with your precious story,' he said, his eyes coldly impassive now. 'Reckon I've given you plenty of material—in fact, I congratulate you. You know more about me than any other reporter has ever been able to find out. Should make a hell of an exclusive. What are you going to do with it? Hawk it round Fleet Street for the highest bidder?'

She looked away from his penetrating eyes, miserably aware she had originally intended to do just that.

'You sure worked hard enough to get the story,' he continued unhurriedly. 'Admittedly most of the work was done on your back, of course. Will you tell the readers about that too?'

'Look, it was never meant to be this way,' she cut in desperately, unable to take any more.

'No, I guess it probably wasn't. I imagine you intended to bring the subject up casually one day—just after making love, I'd bet. What were you going to say, Leigh? "Oh, by the way, Ross darling, could you just tell me what it's like being a superstar while we're lying here with nothing better to do?"' He cruelly mocked her voice, then shook his head. 'Sorry, lady, I've dealt with much bigger fish than you. But I'll give you credit for one thing—you did at least try an original scheme. I've never had a reporter crawl into my bed before.'

She was devastated by his scorn, but managed to hold her head high, refusing to look away from his eyes. 'You'll never believe me now,' she said quietly. 'But these past days have been the sweetest of my life.'

'Then enjoy the memory, moonlight lady. Because that's all you'll ever have.' He turned on his heel and walked out of the kitchen. Seconds later she heard the front door slam and knew he'd gone out of her life for ever. She could have run after him—could have tried to force him to listen—but she dismissed the idea as soon as it occurred. She had known from the start the island fantasy with Ross could never be any more than just that—had always known it was bound to end as soon as he returned to his real life. Maybe it was even better this way—she had been left with no illusions, no false hopes. She wouldn't have to face an eternity of waiting for letters or phone calls that never came—wouldn't have to cope with any fake promises from him that he never intended to keep.

Moving painfully slowly, she went back upstairs to the bedroom, the tears starting in her eyes as she took in the unmade bed, saw the notebook lying on the floor where he had flung it in his fury. The pillow still bore the imprint of his head and she flung herself down on to the bed, breathing in the fragrance lingering on the sheets. It was all she had left of him.

Leigh stood by the open window, absent-mindedly knotting a scarf about her throat as she breathed in the fresh, cool morning air. Considering what lay before her, she felt remarkably calm. Somehow she knew it was up to her to seek Ross out—that he wouldn't make the first move to come to her. Well, she had finally faced up to the painful memories after so many years of shutting them out of her mind, had lain for hours in the darkness letting the images play before her mind's eye, and in a strange way she felt better—somehow cleansed, as though she had gone through some sort of bloodletting ceremony. Perhaps she should have faced up to it all a long time ago, she acknowledged, bending over to pull on a pair of flat leather boots over her red corduroy trousers. Surely nothing else could ever in her life be as shattering as the anguish she had gone through five years before—and since she had survived that, she could survive whatever else he had in store for her.

She cast a last look over the bedroom before making her way downstairs—nothing there to show the kind of soul-searching night she had just gone through, just a tidy, pretty room with a big old bed and pillows that showed no trace of having been hugged close when the tears threatened to become overwhelming. Now it was up to her to present the same kind of unruffled image to him.

She left the cottage without bothering to lock the door—at this off-season time of year when few tourists were around, there was little need for the kind of precautions she would automatically have taken in the city. She walked briskly down the path to Ross's cottage, enjoying the sharp bite of the cold winter air, letting her eyes fill with the beauty of the landscape. If it hadn't been for all the memories the place held she would have been back years ago, she admitted silently. The island had never lost its hold on her heart, even though she had shut that fact away with the rest of those debilitating pictures.

She wasn't surprised to find the cottage empty—she hadn't really expected him to make things easy for her. It didn't matter—there was no rush, and anyway, she had a fair idea where he would be. She turned away from the door and headed along the path leading to the beach cove.

She spotted him as soon as she set foot on the sand—a dark figure at the end of the cove, unmoving and apparently unaware of her presence. She trudged along the shore, the sounds of waves and calling seagulls sounding unnaturally loud in her ears. When she reached his side she stood for a long moment looking down at him, watching him sleep, and her heart was washed over by sadness. She had almost forgotten the way he looked in sleep—so young and carefree, the lines of pain and experience all but smoothed away. Since she had seen him in London, he had dyed his hair again, she noticed—now he looked exactly like the Ross she had known. In sleep he had so often held her close, never allowing her to move too far away, seeming to need her there even in his dreams. She remembered the many times she had lain awake, deliberately keeping sleep at bay, wishing only to prolong the hours spent in his arms. Seeing him this way was almost more painful than hearing his words of accusation and scorn, yet she could have watched him for hours. Carefully she knelt at his side, tucking her long legs under her, the soft sounds of his breathing bringing a fresh ache—she hadn't expected to be so close to him as he slept ever again. It couldn't last, of course—unhappily she gazed away over the white-tipped waves, steeling herself for the inevitable moment when he would awake and all the anger would begin again.

'Hi.' The tiny word whispered over her and she turned to see him watching her, his tawny eyes soft and warm. 'I wondered when you'd get here.' The words, a perfect repeat of the ones she had used the first time she had seen him, brought tears to her eyes and she blinked them hastily away, terrified he would notice her moment of weakness. She began to speak, but the words were stilled when he took her arm and gently pulled her down beside him.

'Ross, I...'

'Hush, mermaid,' he murmured, and his hand buried itself in her hair, guiding her head down to lie against his shoulder. The move was so unexpected and yet seemed so right, she could do no other than simply nestle against him, unresisting, hearing a strange wild singing somewhere in her mind.

'Don't say anything,' he crooned against her hair. 'Just lie for a moment and keep me warm.'

The moment was as brief and as beautiful as a butterfly's lifespan, and just as fragile. She could have lain there for ever, feeling the strength of him, drinking in the warm male scent of him, her senses reeling as his fingers gently stroked her neck. But his unexpected tenderness was robbing her of the defences she had so carefully constructed, leaving her open and vulnerable all over again, and she couldn't allow that to happen, not if she cherished any hope of getting out of this thing with her sanity intact. She pushed herself out of his embrace, unable to face his eyes as she sat up, brushing the tumbling golden hair away from her flushed face.

'Why did you do that, Slade?' she said quietly.

'God knows.' She flinched at the hollowness of his voice, but forced herself to look at him. His eyes, the same amber as fine old whisky, glittered with hostility. 'Maybe I thought there was just a remote chance the enchantment of this place could still reach you—if there was still anything left within you that was honest and open enough to be reached. But then, perhaps there never was. Perhaps I only ever imagined there was a warm, loving person beneath the self-seeking career-minded journalist. Obviously I was wrong.'

She bit back the words of protest that sprang to her tongue. Somehow she had to keep things clear in her mind—she was here to do a job, and then get back to London and her own life as soon as possible. For her own sake she couldn't afford to let him complicate matters all over again—no matter how desperately she might long to. She focused on a single gull far above in the overcast sky, wheeling on the wind currents, wishing she could rise up and fly as easily.

'I've done as you asked,' she finally found her voice. 'Or rather—as you demanded. I've tracked you down. I take it you will now honour your side of the bargain.'

He laughed harshly. 'So you're not even going to try to conceal what you really want this time. Perhaps I should applaud you for that—it's honest if nothing else. You should have tried the same tactics when you met me the first time.'

'And told you I was a journalist?' She whipped round to face him, her blue eyes sparking silver fire. 'Had I done so, I'd have been allowed the dubious pleasure of your company for precisely thirty seconds.' Her lips narrowed to a thin line. 'So maybe you're right—heaven knows it would have been better in the long run.'

'You think so?' His voice mocked her. 'Better for whom?'

'Better for me.' She spoke slowly, afraid of the anger building up inside. 'I don't imagine the revelation had any lasting traumatic effect on you—except perhaps to dent your massive pride a tiny bit. You were so damn convinced I was only interested in your famous *alter ego*, nothing short of a mountain landslide could have persuaded you otherwise.'

'Because it was the truth. Come on, Leigh, after all this time, can't you just admit to it?'

'Just what do you want me to say?' The words were ripped from her. 'Yes, Slade, it was you I wanted all along—Ross Stuart was merely an obstacle on the way—an irritation I had to pander to?'

He nodded slowly. 'I guess that just about sums it up. But in any case, you seem to have coped with it all pretty well. Better than that, judging by the job you've got now—so even if things didn't go as you originally planned, you obviously managed to turn them to your advantage. Which is what I'd have expected.'

She gazed down at the pebble she was rolling in her fingers, vaguely wondering when she had picked it up. None of this was going as she had planned—she'd intended to stay calm and rational, to maintain a cool façade no matter what he said or did. Instead, she had reacted like a tinder-box, going up in flames at his goading—and there was no better way to betray her own weakness. Somehow she had to get back on to an even keel.

'Look,' she strove for a tone of sensible reasoning, 'this is ridiculous. It'll do neither of us any good whatsoever to rake over old coals. I think we should both forget what happened between us in the past—we're here now for one reason and one reason only—the interview for *She Speaks*. My editor doesn't even know I've followed you here, but she'll be expecting results shortly. Frankly I don't have the time to waste in verbal jousting. So I'd be very grateful if we could just get through with this as quickly as possible, then go our separate ways.'

'Is it really so awful being with me again, Leigh?' The softness in his voice and in his eyes effectively shattered the slender shield she'd started to raise, and for a second she could do nothing but gaze at him, unconsciously parting her lips in an unspoken plea. Then she stiffened—the man was an actor, for goodness sake, this was probably a scene he had played a hundred times. And she was on the verge of being fool enough to fall for it. 'That's not what I meant,' she said coldly. 'But I stand by what I said—it can't benefit either of us to drag up past history all over again.'

'I wouldn't worry about your editor.' He took the pebble from her fingers and tossed it far out into the sea. 'I told her not to expect you around for a few days.' He grinned. 'I got the distinct impression that she wouldn't be at all unhappy about that. What's the matter there, Leigh—isn't she one of your legion of devoted admirers?'

She stared at him in amazement. 'No, she's not. And she'll be less friendly still if I don't turn in a good story after all this. What do you mean, you told her not to expect me around?'

'Just what I said. Your Miss Bell-Rowley or whatever she calls herself is no fool—in fact I couldn't help wondering if she's really just an older version of you. She's got an eye to the main chance, that one. She knows an exclusive with me is bound to sell more of her precious magazines, so she's prepared to play ball with me.'

The suggestion that she could ever be like Christine Bell-Reilly would have struck Leigh as comical under any other circumstances. But coming from him, it hurt her to the quick—was that really how he saw her? The fast retort died in her throat as she realised it probably was—and that perhaps he had, in his own mind at least, good reason to see her in the same light as the coldly calculating, ruthless editor-in-chief of *She Speaks*.

'And did she say anything else I should know about, since she didn't deign to pass on this information to me?' asked Leigh acidly.

He shrugged. 'Why should she? You're simply her employee—I'm the prize catch.'

For two pins she would have hit him, just swung round on the spot and smacked the grin from his face. His eyes glittered, challenging her.

'Go on,' he said softly. 'I dare you.'

She gripped her hands fiercely in her lap, refusing to let them have their way, and stared stonily back at him. 'I don't know what you mean.'

'You do disappoint me. I never took you for a coward—or is it just that you're afraid of losing the story? Why don't you just let fly, Leigh? You know you want to.'

You'll never know how much, she swore silently, venom flashing in her silvery eyes. Just what was it about this man that stung her so easily to temper? He seemed to know just how to light the fuse—knew the weak points to probe till she could barely contain herself any longer. It was simply another thing she would have to battle against in her dealings with him.

'So, Mr Keller,' she said evenly, 'what was it exactly that made you want to be a film star in the first place?'

She spotted a fleeting glimmer of admiration in his eyes and mentally awarded herself a point. It was good to know she could score some victories in this all-out war—no matter how slight.

'It's not the most original question I've ever heard,' he drawled, and she gritted her teeth, refusing to let her tiny moment of triumph be taken away. 'But I guess it's as good a start as any. Got your notebook?'

'I prefer to use this.' She pulled a small cassette recorder from her shoulder bag and flicked the rewind switch to send the tape back to the start.

'Shorthand not so hot, huh?'

She opened her mouth to retort, then laughed, unable to resist the teasing expression on his face.

'You could say that,' she conceded. 'Anyway, this is more accurate—and it gives me a permanent record of what someone's said, should there be any comeback at a later date.'

'Do people often complain about what you've written?' he asked curiously. 'Perhaps you'd better give me a little warning here of what to expect.'

'I never deliberately misquote them if that's what you mean. But of course, people are occasionally unhappy to see things in print they'd rather have kept hidden.'

'So why not let those things remain hidden? Don't people deserve that much privacy?' The amber-brown eyes bored into her. 'Or are you just naturally a gutter-raker?'

She flinched, stung by the change in his tone. 'Some people don't deserve privacy,' she answered briefly, seeing in her mind's eye the last scoop she had delivered up to *She Speaks*—an exposé of an avaricious London landlord who was making fast bucks out of tenants who couldn't afford anything better than the slum conditions he provided. It had been just the type of story that gave her the most satisfaction—laying bare the sordid details of society's most cruel and vicious. She felt sure the story she had planned on the religious sect would have been just as successful, and it still rankled to know Josephine had been handed the assignment.

'I guess that's just the answer I should have expected from someone like you.' She blinked in surprise at the sudden ice in his voice. 'Maybe I'm simply shocked that you should be so blatant about it.'

'Blatant?' She stared at him uncomprehendingly. 'But it's my job to...'

'To dig in the dirt. Yeah, I know.' He shook his head disgustedly. 'And I bet those angel looks take them in every time, don't they, sister?'

She didn't answer, still confused by his lightning change of mood. Minutes before he had seemed almost affable—now his eyes were hard, his words dripping contempt. Surely, even with his well known loathing for the Press, even he could acknowledge the need for people like her—people who weren't afraid to shine a public light on dark dealings that needed to be made known? Or was he so blinkered that he simply saw all journalists as a bad lot, refusing to acknowlege the good work so many did? If so, she had little chance of getting through to him on any kind of level.

Sighing heavily she fingered the cold black casing of the tape recorder. 'Do you want to do this now, or would you prefer to wait till later? Maybe you'd rather we talked indoors, somewhere more comfortable.'

'Not at all. You may be accustomed to doing your work in more luxurious surroundings, but this suits me.'

'Fine.' She reined in her impatience with a visible effort and pressed the start switch on the recorder, angling it towards the man sprawled so casually by her side. 'Tell me a bit about your childhood first.'

'You know about my childhood,' he said shortly. 'Or has your memory erased all that? Wasn't it important enough for you to hold on to?'

'Look, Slade, you told those things to me as a friend, not a journalist.' The impatience was beginning to rise in her again, but she managed to bite it back. 'I'm not about to use anything you told me then, it wouldn't be fair under the circumstances. So I'd much rather you just start all over again and talk to me as if we'd never met before.'

'I'm beginning to wonder if we ever really did.' He raised himself up on one elbow to scrutinise her. 'Or is this all part of the game, I wonder—what are you trying to do here exactly? Con me into believing there's a shred of integrity there after all?'

Biting her lip, Leigh stopped the recorder. No point in wasting tape and batteries on this. 'Look, just how many times do I have to apologise for what happened five years ago?'

His eyes glittered strangely. 'I'm not aware that you've apologised at all yet. I sure haven't heard the word "sorry", unless I'm going deaf.'

She stared at him in horror, realising for the first time that he was speaking the truth. She really hadn't apologised—she had been so much on the defensive ever since meeting him again, so convinced he would never listen to her. 'Well, maybe I didn't use the word because I knew you'd never hear it,' she said at last.

'Or more likely that you didn't mean it.' His eyes flickered over her. 'The only thing you were sorry about was that your little plan didn't work—that I tumbled to you just a little bit too soon. Isn't that the truth of it, Leigh?'

'No, it damn well isn't.' She clambered slowly to her feet. 'But I'm not going to waste any more time trying to convince you of that. You've got a mental block where I'm concerned, Slade—I can't hope to do an interview with you while it's there, while you're more concerned with scoring points than talking to me honestly and openly. And I'm not at all sure it's worth the effort anyway.' Without a backward look she turned away, striding off down the beach with her head held high, refusing to react when his laughter followed her on the wind.

CHAPTER SEVEN

SHE spent the rest of the morning alone, just walking and going over in her mind all that had happened earlier. His actions on the beach still confused her—just what had he been trying to achieve by pulling her into his arms and holding her so close? Had it been a deliberate attempt to lull her into some kind of a false sense of friendship before throwing it all back in her face? He seemed so hell-bent on revenge, it must be possible. And yet—his hands had been so gentle, his murmuring words so soft—could they really have been nothing more than a ploy? She shook herself mentally, annoyed at her own wishful thinking—this was probably all part of one big master plan—maybe even designed to get her back into his bed, for whatever else she was unsure of, she was certain of one thing—that he still wanted her in a purely physical sense. It showed in his eyes when he looked at her, shone through the way his body moved. She remembered writing an article a couple of years back on so-called body language, the theory that people said a great deal just by the way they stood, or sat, or gestured. At the time she had been intrigued by the idea, but not wholly convinced. Now she was forced to think again. Slade was displaying all the signs of a man holding himself in check—but only just. As for herself—she only had to think of that humiliating scene back in his London hotel bedroom to know she was still a pushover where he was concerned. He had had a power over her five years before that hadn't diminished with time. Even in the midst of arguing with him, resenting him, coming near to hating him, she still longed for him with a passion that was all but overwhelming.

Vaguely thinking she might call in to see Jack at the restaurant, she walked the two miles or so to the village, barely noticing the distance as the thoughts danced in her mind. But when she reached Lochranza and saw a closed sign on the shop door, she was almost relieved. She wasn't really in the mood for company—and Jack's friendly brown eyes had a disconcerting habit of seeing right through her. Much as she liked the great bear of a man, she wasn't ready to spill out her heart to him.

She crossed the road and walked down to the tiny tumbledown castle on the shore, glad to see it was deserted. She had always had a soft spot in her memory for this place—not much more now than four crumbling walls. The castle in Brodick, the island's main village, was a much more impressive affair, standing out sturdily against the backdrop of Goatfell mountain. She had never been inside, but she had seen pictures of its lavishly furnished rooms, and she knew there were regular guided tours in the summer months. Once, she and Ross had cycled up to the castle and wandered hand in hand through its vast beautiful gardens, content to imagine what the place would look like in the full glory of summer, but happy to have it to themselves. Afterwards they had ridden back along the long winding drive, whooping and shouting like children when they hit a downhill stretch. Leigh had told him she felt like Katharine Ross in *Butch Cassidy and the Sundance Kid* in the famous scene where she and Paul Newman take a bike ride. Ross's eyes had narrowed at that and she had bitten her tongue, scared she had made him suspicious by mentioning the film world, but she had managed to laugh her way out of it, teasingly telling him he would make a great Sundance with his Mexican moustache.

She leaned against one of the thick outer walls, letting her eyes roam over the gentle waves of the bay. Even though Brodick Castle was grand and elegant, she would always prefer this old place, she thought distantly, it somehow pulled at her heart-strings, standing there so proudly with all its memories.

'This is where my grandparents did their courting.'

The voice filtered through her thoughts and she looked up to see Ross walking across the grass towards her.

'They used to tell me stories about the castle when I was a kid,' he went on, reaching her side. 'I had a picture of it in my mind, clear as could be.'

'Were you disappointed when you saw it for the first time?' she asked softly, feeling a strange warmth creep into her veins. No matter what happened between them, she couldn't ever deny the tremor of joy she felt whenever he appeared.

'Disappointed?' He looked down at her questioningly. 'No, I wasn't. It was just the way I'd pictured it—small and old and weather-beaten.' He grinned. 'A bit like my grandfather in fact.'

'Small?' The description surprised her. It was hard to imagine Ross with his six-foot-plus height having any diminutive relatives.

'Well, I guess he wasn't so small when he was a young man,' Ross looked pensive. 'But all the years of hard work took their toll on him.'

'Is that why you chose such a different way of life?'

He shot her a grin. 'Because I couldn't cope with hard work, you mean? If anyone else suggested that I'd slug them. No, that wasn't the reason.' His eyes grew thoughtful. 'Given the choice I'd probably have stayed on the ranch all my life—never ventured much further than the next state.'

'So what happened?' It was something she had always been curious about.

'Got your recorder ready, reporter lady?' He looked at her with something like amusement. 'You never let up, do you, Leigh? You're a journalist to the backbone, always quick with the questions.'

'Can't I simply ask because I'm interested in the answers for their own sake?' she said hotly, annoyed that he had misinterpreted her again.

He shrugged. 'I guess so—but it's all good material. You can't be unaware of that.'

'I'm not. But I wouldn't use anything you didn't want me to—I give you my word on that.'

'Is that an understanding you give to everyone you interview?' His expression clearly said he didn't believe a word of it, and she hesitated before answering.

'No, quite frankly it's not, but...'

'I thought not. So don't bother trying to soft-soap me, Leigh—I've been taken in before by smooth-talking reporters, but it won't ever happen again.'

'Look, Ross, I mean Slade,' she bit her lips at the unthinking slip of the tongue. 'No matter what you think of me, I'm not a member of the gutter Press. I've never knowingly published something just for the hell of it. If you'd ever read any of my articles, you'd know that what I write, I write for good reasons. And I do respect other people's privacy—I don't go snooping through keyholes or rummaging in dustbins.'

'Or reading other people's notebooks?' He chuckled softly. 'Guess I deserved that.'

'I didn't mean that,' she said stiffly, stabbed to the heart by the easy, flippant way he had dismissed an event which had proved catastrophic in her life. Obviously it hadn't meant a can of beans to him. 'Anyway, would you object to me using any details about your background in the article?' Somehow she had to get back on course, since veering off it only led her into dangerous territory.

He shook his head. 'No. Only don't go painting me as some kind of home-town hero, or I'll deny every word.'

She sighed heavily. In all the time she had been working as an investigative journalist, she had never come across anyone as wary as him. Trying to pin him down was like trying to catch a moth in an empty barn.

'Why don't you just tell me the story,' she said evenly. 'I won't do anything to colour the readers' opinions—they can make up their own minds.' She fished the recorder out of her bag and held it towards him. 'Just talk. I won't alter so much as a comma, I promise you.'

His eyes measured her for a moment, then he grinned. 'OK. Ask away.'

She took a deep breath. 'Was it a childhood ambition of yours to be an actor?'

He leaned back against the stone wall, considering his reply. 'No, ma'am. In fact you could probably say it was the furthest thing from my mind. I had a fine, healthy childhood—I grew up with good people in a good country, surrounded by animals and fields, and folks who felt just the way I did, that cities were strange, alien places we had no need for.' He smiled softly, remembering. 'I even felt sorry for the people who had to live there. I thought it must be some sort of hell.'

'So what happened to change all that?'

'Guess you could say fate took a hand in it all.' His eyes darkened, and she saw the shadows of pain in the amber depths. 'Fate in the shape of the Vietnam war, that is.' He shot her a quick, warning look. 'And don't go asking me about that, because I've got nothing to say. But for the record, I came back a different person—and I found I couldn't settle to the ranch again.'

'Why not?' She almost whispered the question, afraid to deflect his train of thought. She had forgotten the tape recorder in her hand—sensing that he was opening up to her, perhaps for the first time.

He lifted his shoulders. 'It was too beautiful, too clean and real. I don't imagine you'll understand any of this, but I felt dirty, unworthy of the people back home. I hadn't done anything in Vietnam to be so desperately ashamed of—but war's a filthy game, and for a while I couldn't cope with the memories of it all—at least, not on the ranch where there was too much time to think.' He was gazing down at the ground, unthinkingly scuffing his heel against a rock. 'So I went to New York—thought I could lose myself in the crowds for a while.' He smiled, but there was no warmth in his eyes. 'And I did lose myself—I nearly lost my mind in that crazy city—no place for a country boy, I can tell you,' he said self-mockingly, and she longed to reach out to him, to smooth away the lines of pain on his face. 'Then an old army buddy found me—more or less dragged me out of the mire I'd gotten myself into. To cut a long, long story short, he got me back on my feet again, and all but shoved me along in front of him. He'd been an actor before going over to 'Nam, and he still had a lot of contacts in the business—well, he kinda took me under his wing, saw something in me he thought the film-makers could use. He got me a few auditions, helped me land a couple of screen roles in cigarette adverts—and a director spotted me. The rest is common knowledge, I guess—the first film did well, the second better still, and my career took off like a rocket after that.' He paused, choosing his words carefully. 'I think I took to acting naturally because it gave me the escape I'd been looking for—allowed me to portray different people, wear different masks, and to shove my own identity into the background.'

Leigh's heart ached for the mental anguish he had so clearly suffered—pain of a sort she couldn't even begin to imagine. His revelations had taken her completely by surprise—not simply because he had made them, but because in doing so he had revealed a depth of vulnerability in his make-up that few people could be aware of. She had to clear her throat before she could speak, pushing the words through lips grown suddenly dry. 'How did you finally manage to come to terms with yourself?' she said softly.

'What makes you so sure I have?' He eyed her evenly, then gave a little half-smile. 'It took a while—I could have gone to an analyst, I guess, that's the usual route in the States. But I didn't want to do that—I wanted to find the answers for myself, and I think I did, or some of them at least. The thing that helped me most was the film I did about Vietnam.'

She drew in her breath sharply. She knew the film he was talking about, had seen it several times, and marvelled at the brilliance of his acting, even as she shuddered at the horrors the film portrayed. 'Wasn't that tough on you?' she said carefully.

'No more tough than on any of the other veterans playing alongside me. But in a sense it was a catharsis—oh, it was only a film, just make-believe, but in a strange way, it helped me to face up to the things I'd been shutting away in a dark corner of my mind.' He stood in silence for a moment, then angled his head to look at her, his eyes strangely bleak. 'And then a reporter came along—he thought it would be a fine idea to compare the part I played in the film with the real version of what I'd done in 'Nam. Only the things I told him apparently weren't good enough—he wanted tales of blood and guts and macho-men striding through battlefields. So he did what reporters through the ages have always done—he made up the facts to suit himself. When the story hit the paper, I was made out to be the big hero, the man with notches on his gun.' His voice tailed away as he stared away over the blue water of the bay. When he spoke again, his words were clipped, bitter. 'If I'd found the guy, I might have killed him—not for what he'd done to me, but for the damage he'd done to all those other wounded spirits who came back from that hell-hole all too well aware of their own failures.' He twisted round to look at her and she steeled herself not to look away from the accusation in his eyes. 'Not long after that, I came over here to the island.'

'And met me.' She whispered the words, the full weight of what he was saying suddenly sinking in on her. 'And you thought I would turn out to be just like that other reporter.' She felt the sting of tears behind her eyes but made no attempt to blink them away. 'Oh, God, Ross, I'm so sorry. You came here looking for something, and I ruined that dream for you.'

For a long moment he looked at her, taking in the tell-tale glimmer turning her eyes to silver. He lifted his hand and for a breathless second she thought he was about to reach out to her, but at the last moment he changed his mind and his hand dropped back to his side. 'It was my own fault in a way,' he said evenly. 'I'd listened to the old folks' tales for so long, I began to believe this island really was enchanted—I thought I'd find something here that perhaps doesn't even exist any more.'

'I wish I'd known then,' she said sadly.

'And what would you have done? Jumped into my bed a little faster to help me get over the nightmares?' His lips twisted cynically. 'Don't go all wounded heart on me now, Leigh, it doesn't ring true. It was my bad fortune that I should go straight from one lying skunk of a journalist to another, that's all.'

'I didn't lie to you,' she cried, lacerated by his scorn. 'You never gave me the chance to explain—and now I'm forever branded in your eyes because of what another reporter did to you. Whatever you may think, we're not all alike.'

'That's true,' he nodded slowly, never taking his eyes from her. 'At least you paid me for my story with your body—he never tried to do anything of the kind.'

'Look.' She faced him squarely, wondering wildly how the force of his anger had once again come to be turned upon her. 'It's obvious you'll never believe a word I say—but why must you keep dredging it up all over again? I can't undo the things that happened between us—especially since you won't even let me try. Why don't we just start all over, as if we'd never met before, and forget the past?

That way I can be Leigh Daniels, magazine journalist, and you can be Slade Keller, film star—all very precise and clear, with no misconceptions on either side. I can then do the interviews I need to without being afraid every time I open my mouth that you'll slam me down all over again for something that happened between us a very long time ago.'

'Then you can leave Arran and take your precious story back to your editor and forget the whole thing?'

She lifted her eyes to his face, expecting to find the coldly cynical look she was coming to recognise only too well. Instead he was smiling, his eyes crinkled in amusement.

'That's about it, yes,' she said slowly, wondering if she was about to fall headlong into another trap.

He shrugged. 'Seems like you're asking a lot—just to wipe away the past as if it never happened.' Then he nodded. 'Maybe you're right though. Maybe it really is the only way we can communicate without biting each other's heads off every few minutes. In any case,' he swivelled slowly to face her, his eyes showing no emotion whatsoever, 'why should we keep harking back in time? After all, there's nothing in the past either of us wants to remember. Is there?'

She swallowed hard against the instinctive denial rising in her throat. Nothing she wanted to remember? What about the glorious times they had shared before the bitterness swamped all else? What about the times they had laughed together, held each other, made love? Feeling as though she was betraying her best friend, she slowly shook her head. 'No, there's nothing.'

For just a second there was a flicker of something she couldn't put a name to in his tawny eyes. Then he nodded. 'That's what I thought you'd say. Well, if that's the case, we should drink a toast to new beginnings.'

'A toast?' she regarded him quizzically. 'With what?'

'With a coffee from Jack's restaurant.' He nodded over towards the little café. 'I saw him going in there a little while ago, and I'm sure he'll spare time from his cooking to brew a couple of cups for his old friends.' Then he chuckled, realising his own mistake. 'I mean, for the two complete strangers who are about to descend upon him.'

CHAPTER EIGHT

If Leigh had ever had any doubts about Slade Keller's acting abilities, the next couple of days would have banished them utterly. Having set the role for himself, he maintained it with never a slip, never betraying by even the flicker of an eyelash that the whole thing was no more than a sham. At first she admired him for that—especially since she was finding it hard going herself. Several times she had to bite her lips to silence unthinking references to the past, and when they revisited old haunts, it became an absolute agony to keep pretending they had never been there together before. And even though the whole thing had been her idea in the first place, there were times when she was all but consumed by frustration—wanted to yell at him to stop being so damn clever and let the real Ross show through for a second. But she gritted her teeth and held fast to her determination to see the thing through.

The irony of the whole situation didn't escape her either. Here they were, five years on, both playing different roles—he was secure in his portrayal of his other self—she was trying hard to pretend she was no more to him than Leigh Daniels, magazine journalist. And after all, why should it be difficult for him? she asked herself more than once. He was simply playing himself—perhaps being more genuine in that than he had been five years before. Perhaps she really had fallen in love then with a man who no longer really existed—perhaps this urbane, charming stranger was the real person now. But oh, how she longed for just a glimpse of the old laughing, spontaneous Ross—just a tiny flicker to convince her he hadn't gone for ever.

She could certainly have no complaints about his co-operation as far as the interviews were concerned—he answered her every question with apparent willingness, amused her with outrageous tales of life on the film set, showed no reluctance to open up to her probing. The article would be a winner, of that she had no doubt. So why did she feel so strangely empty and unsatisfied? It was turning out, after the unpromising beginning, to be one of the easiest assignments she had ever tackled, yet she couldn't shake off the feeling that she was only scraping the surface of the man—that there was much more there he wasn't allowing her access to. That frustrated her as a journalist—but on a personal level, it was driving her slowly demented, even though she kept telling herself it was really all for the best. This, after all, was what she'd wanted, surely? An easy ride, with none of the old friction to get in the way?

They had been together on the island for almost a week when she finally decided she had done enough—had enough on the tapes and in her notebook to satisfy even Christine Bell-Reilly. Slade, still sporting what he laughingly called his 'island disguise' of moustache and dyed hair, had refused to be photographed, but had willingly agreed to a photo session back in London at the end of it all. So, she told herself, that was it. There was no more to be said, no more questions to be asked, no more stories to be told. She could go home at last, write the article, then forget the whole thing. Slade could return to his world, and never give another thought to the young female reporter who had once upon a time cried his name aloud in the darkness of night—the whole episode could now be laid to rest, and not before time. It was only her own silly head that insisted there should be much more to it than this.

At the end of their last session together, when he had patiently gone over the details of his first-ever film contract once again for her, she switched the tape recorder off with a flourish, and turned to him with a beaming smile that somehow didn't quite reach her eyes.

'Well, I reckon that's it,' she said brightly. 'The readers of *She Speaks* should be queuing up to buy the next issue. I want to thank you for your co-operation, Slade—you've really been helpful and I do appreciate it.'

'Then cook a meal for me tonight.' His tone was off-handedly casual, but his eyes held something she couldn't quite analyse.

'A meal?' The request confused her. She had been so sure he would jump at the chance to say a final farewell to her. 'We could go to Jack's place if you're intending to stay another night. I had thought you'd probably leave as soon as the interviews were over.'

'I'm in no rush,' he said evenly. 'And I'm sure your editor can do without you for one more day. But I don't feel like having other people around.' The look in his amber-brown eyes sent a strange shiver along her spine. 'Just this one last night—let's make it just you and me—OK?'

She found herself nodding. 'OK,' she whispered. She forced a smile to lips that were suddenly quivering for no good reason. 'If you can cope with my cooking, that is.'

'I never had any problems with it before.' It was the first time in days that he had made any reference to the past, and she was forced to swallow hard.

'Come round to the cottage about eight o'clock.' She heard the tremor in her own voice, wondered if it was apparent to him too. He made no sign of having heard it, for he simply nodded.

'I'll bring the champagne.'

She told herself she wouldn't go to any trouble—he would simply have to take pot luck. So he was accustomed to glitzy Hollywood suppers with the *hautest* of *haute cuisine*—too bad. After all, he had invited himself for dinner—he would just have to accept whatever she could rustle up at such short notice.

She was still telling herself that when she slid into a lavishly perfumed bath, cursing softly as she looked at her watch. She should never have let Jack talk her into cooking such a complicated meal. The whole afternoon had been a rush—even though the kitchen cupboards were well stocked with essentials, there was nothing there to conjure a proper meal out of—and she could hardly serve up toast and cheese, no matter how casual she wanted the evening to be.

After she had left Slade, she had walked to the village, intending to ask Jack if she could borrow his car for a quick trip to Brodick where the stores had more of a choice than the Lochranza village shop. But when he had heard about the dinner, he had promptly turned to his own fridge, and presented her with two beautiful fillet steaks. Then, even as she protested that she only wanted to do something simple, he filled a basket with vegetables and home-made paté.

'You know how to make pastry, don't you?' He cut into her words as if she hadn't even spoken. 'I'll write down the instructions for you, but basically what you have to do is stuff the steaks with the paté, then put the lot into pastry envelopes.' He rolled his eyes appreciatively. 'It's called Steak Wellington—a little bit fiddly perhaps, but well worth the effort.' He smiled at her affectionately. 'And after all, you do know the way to a man's heart is through his stomach.'

'I've already told you it's nothing like that,' she said stiffly. 'I simply promised to cook a meal at the cottage as a way of saying thank you for all the help he's given me. I've got no desire to get to his heart by any route.'

'No?' Jack slid her a sideways look. 'Then just spoil yourself. It's a wonderful meal.' He carefully placed a container of luscious red strawberries on top of the basket and slid a carton of cream in beside them. 'They just arrived on the ferry this morning,' he remarked casually. 'I've got a supplier on the mainland who lets me have the very best of out of season fruit.'

'Jack, why are you doing this?' she said helplessly.

He grinned. 'God knows. I must be a hopeless old romantic at heart. Or maybe just plain hopeless.'

She reached up to kiss his cheek. 'You're a fine man,' she said softly. 'And a good friend, even if your brains are addled. How much do I owe you for this little lot?'

'Owe me?' He pretended to be scandalised. 'Out of here, woman, before I chase you with my rolling pin.'

'But...'

'But nothing.' He eyed her sternly. 'Friends never "owe" each other anything, don't you know that?'

His words came back to her as she clambered out of the bath and headed for the bedroom. Whatever he believed, she knew she owed him a great deal—for simply being there, a kindly, comforting presence in the midst of all the confusion. Why on earth couldn't she have lost her heart to this straightforward, generous man—instead of a great ox like Ross Stuart with all his hang-ups and complications? Because, as a friend of hers had once succinctly put it, love was a bitch. She grinned at the thought—not exactly a lyrical phrase perhaps, but oh, so true. Then she spotted the little clock on the bedside table and gave an anguished yelp—just ten minutes to go and she hadn't even dressed yet. Everything else fled her mind as she tussled with the problem of what to wear—not that it really mattered of course, she reminded herself—she wasn't dressing to impress. In any case, the limited selection of clothes she had brought with her didn't exactly afford a lot of choice in the matter—it was either jeans and a sweatshirt, or the one and only dress she had packed. She held it against her, surveying her reflection in the mirror—why in the name of all that was wonderful had she taken it along anyway? Why hadn't she packed something sober and suitable? Because she hadn't had much time to think about it, she reasoned, and anyway, this dress had always been a particular favourite. She could always depend on its softly flowing lines to show off her figure to its best advantage, and the dusky pink colours brought out a warmth in her fair skin. But it was undoubtedly a rather sexy little number, with its plunging back and side slit—not at all the image she was looking for tonight. She was about to fling it back into the suitcase and opt for the jeans instead, when something stopped her. Why on earth shouldn't she look her very best—why should she dress down? Wouldn't that be, in its own way, an admission of cowardice? No, to hell with it, she would wear the dress—if nothing else, it would give her a feeling of self-confidence she could well do with. As a compromise to her conscience, she wouldn't bother with make-up, other than a flick of mascara and a mere dab of lipstick, maybe just a tiny touch of blusher to counteract her natural paleness. The perfume she sprayed on her wrists was simply a finishing touch, the extra squirt behind the ears just for good luck.

Minutes later she stood before the front door, wishing to heaven she had opted for the jeans. The dress was supposed to give her self-confidence—instead its material clinging to her body made her feel as naked as a mermaid lying in all her splendour on an empty beach. Well, it was way too late to do anything about it now. She took a deep, steadying breath and opened the door—only to feel as if all the stuffing had been knocked clean out of her when she saw him standing in the doorway. For the first time since she had known him he wasn't wearing blue jeans, but beautifully cut dark grey trousers and jacket, crisp white shirt and dark red tie. He had never looked more gorgeous, she thought hazily, nor more unapproachable. This stunning male creature was far removed from the laughing-eyed companion who had once been such a frequent visitor to this very cottage.

Lord, where had that errant thought come from? After all the hard work she had put in over the past few days to convince herself Ross Stuart had never been anything more than a figment of her imagination—the last thing she needed was for the memories to come flooding back now. Not when she just had one more evening to get through. With a supreme effort she managed to summon up a smile and held out her hand.

'Welcome, Slade,' she said with a calmness she was far from feeling. 'You're bang on time.'

His eyebrows quirked questioningly. 'Slade? Sorry ma'am, guess there must be some mistake here. I'm Ross Stuart.'

Her mouth fell open at his casual bombshell—just what kind of game was he playing now? He took a single step towards her and she backed hastily away, her heart beating a rapid tattoo in her breast.

'Don't be silly, Slade,' she said breathlessly. 'We've only got a few more hours in each other's company—let's not spoil things now.'

'Spoil things?' he pretended to consider the words, his head tilted to one side. 'I don't know what you mean. Unless . . .' his eyes suddenly bored into her, 'unless Slade Keller's managed to sweep you off your feet so much that you can't stand being with the country boy again. Is that it, Leigh? Do you prefer the company of the famous film star?'

The very question would have made her laugh under different circumstances. Prefer Slade to Ross? It was like asking her if she preferred flashing neon lights to a sunlit sky. But she couldn't tell him that—couldn't betray her true feelings now.

'Look,' she strove for a reasonable tone of voice. 'This is a foolish game—we both know that Ross and Slade are one and the same person. Now I don't really mind which name you wish to be called tonight—in fact, you can be Attila the Hun if you really want to test your acting skills.'

He eyed her closely. 'Is that what you think I've been doing these past few days? Acting?'

She shrugged. 'I don't know and I don't really care. But I do know that you've gone out of your way to be helpful and I do appreciate that, as I already told you. If, by announcing yourself as Ross, you're telling me you intend to be difficult this evening, then frankly I'd rather you left right now. I'd prefer to end this thing on a positive note—not with yet another row.'

He grinned, and for just a second she could see a flash of the old impetuous Ross. 'Leave? And sacrifice whatever meal is making that glorious aroma? Not on your life. Now lead me to the kitchen, woman—this champagne needs to chill for a while.'

Bemused by his sudden change of tone, she did as he asked, then poured drinks for them both from the cocktail cabinet.

'You've got a good memory, Leigh,' he said slowly, after tasting the drink. 'You've fixed this just the way I like it. Just the way you used to fix it. Remember?'

The unexpected softness in his eyes left her floundering for a reply. Was he deliberately trying to knock her off balance? But why—what possible good could it achieve?

'There's something I've been meaning to ask you.' She dragged her eyes away from his and sat down on one of the big comfortable armchairs.

'Ask away.' He dropped into the depths of the sofa, casually loosening his tie.

'I'd like to know why you decided to let *She Speaks* have the interview with you, when you've refused so many other magazines.'

'Guess you could say I was simply curious to see what the magazine would make of the story—or, to be more accurate, I wondered how you would tackle it.'

'I see.' She nodded slowly, then a thought struck her and she frowned. 'But how did you find out I was working for the magazine? It's not sold in the States.'

'No, it's not,' he replied. 'But a friend brought back a copy after a trip to Britain. I just happened to flick through it one day—spotted your by-line.'

She was horrified at the sharp stab of jealousy she felt at the casual mention of his 'friend'. Since *She Speaks* was primarily a woman's magazine, it made sense that the friend must surely be female. Had he 'flicked through it' at her place?

'So you've read some of my work?' She forced herself to speak normally.

'I have. And frankly, I didn't think much of it.'

Her eyes flew wide open—had he really set himself so much against her that he couldn't even be honest about her writing? No matter what had happened between them in the past, surely he wasn't that small-minded.

'Just which piece did you read, may I ask,' she said stiltedly.

'It was a rather shabby little gossip column.' His lips twisted in disgust. 'I was surprised even you could sink that low.'

Her heart made a sudden dive right to the soles of her high-heeled shoes. Of all the things he could have read—why did it have to be that awful thing? She had been against the idea of a gossip column from the very start—argued that it would devalue the reputation of the magazine. In fact, that had heralded the start of the war between Bell-Reilly and herself, for she had been features editor then, and the column had been her idea. Fortunately it had only survived for a few months—Leigh had done her best with it, but she just wasn't cut out for the job. She had never been a fan of the traditional gossip writers' favourite haunts—the nightclub scene in London, and the high-society bashes—and she had hated the hypocrisy of people who would ring her up with tasteful little titbits of scandal. In fact, she had used very little of that—preferring to concentrate on harmless pieces of trivia that could harm nobody. Eventually, the then editor had decided to scrap the column, rightly feeling Leigh's talents were being squandered—and in any case, it hadn't proved popular with the readers, many of whom had written in to say they could get that kind of tittle-tattle from the tabloids.

'Which column did you see?' Leigh focused on a patch of carpet, unwilling to meet Slade's eyes. 'Can you remember?'

'Sure I remember. It carried a sordid little piece about an English actor and his latest companion—a not very high-class call-girl as I remember.'

'I didn't write that.' She felt a sudden rush of relief and looked up with a grin. 'That wasn't my piece.'

'It was under your by-line.' The coolness in his voice said he didn't believe her.

'But I didn't write it!' In her eagerness to convince him, she leaned forward, totally unaware that her skirt had parted and she was displaying a healthy portion of thigh. 'I'd been off ill for a few days—when I came back to work, the features editor, the same Miss Bell-Reilly you've spoken to, said the column had been compiled by one of the other reporters.' She gave a little laugh. 'To be honest with you, I was so relieved to have got it off my back, I didn't even bother to check it before it went to press. When I saw it in the magazine, I felt pretty sick. I've never liked that kind of journalism—but by then it was way too late to do anything about it. Fortunately it was all true.'

'Fortunately?' He shot her a look of pure disgust. 'I happen to know the man's marriage broke up because of the revelations in your little column.'

'But that wasn't my fault! Anyway, what I meant was that the magazine could have landed in a great deal of trouble if the allegations had proved to be totally false.'

'And that would have been worse than a broken home?'

She gazed at him in amazement. 'Look, for one thing, that man brought it upon himself—no one forced him to have an affair—and secondly, I don't see why I'm being called upon to defend a story that wasn't even mine!'

'So you say,' he cut in.

'Yes, I damn well do say, because it's true!' She felt her temper begin to rise. 'And if you don't believe me, you need only make a single phone call to my previous editor—he'd tell you the facts as they were.'

'Why don't I simply call Miss Bell-Reilly and ask her?' He eyed her speculatively. 'Wouldn't that be easier?'

Leigh hesitated, biting her bottom lip. With relations the way they were between herself and old Mother Reilly, she couldn't be sure the other woman would come clean. She had landed in hot water over the gossip column issue because she had let another reporter's story be printed under Leigh's name, without Leigh's permission. And the whole office knew she had a memory to rival an elephant's—that little episode probably still rankled. It would be just like her to deny all that Leigh had said.

'I see you're not so keen on that idea,' Slade said heavily, slowly rising to his feet. 'So what's the real story here, Leigh? Did you have a thing going with your old boss? Did you have him twisted round your little finger the way you once tried to twist me? Such a shame your new editor is a woman—not susceptible to your female charms. Must be hard for you to succeed under that sort of regime.'

His unfairness drove her beyond good sense and she got to her feet, facing him with icy coldness, her head tilted proudly back. 'Get out!' She spat the words at him, unbalanced by his unfounded and unjustified accusations. Not for the best exclusive in the world would she put up with this kind of abuse. 'Get out of this cottage now, and don't ever come back. I should have known from the start there was no way we could ever hope to work together—your image of me is so twisted, you couldn't see the truth if it was laid on a platter right at the end of your nose. And I refuse to prostrate myself before you, begging to be heard. If you won't listen to me, there's nothing more I can do to get through to you. So get out.' She turned blindly away, hardly hearing his last muttered words as he made for the door, desperate only to have him leave before the tension building up inside her burst in a flood of tears. Not for anything would she allow him to see her cry—it would be the ultimate humiliation, and no doubt he would love it.

As the door slammed behind her, she picked up a cushion from the chair and flung it blindly at the wall, giving vent to her frustration in a long anguished wail. When the tears came, she dashed them angrily away.

'I've cried enough over you, you heartless bastard!' She screamed the words to the empty room. 'You don't deserve my tears—you're just not worth the pain.'

She caught sight of the dining-table, set for two, the crystal glasses sparkling in the reflected flames of the fire. So much for all the time she had spent labouring over the Steak Wellington! She made her way through to the kitchen and absentmindedly flicked the switch on the wall. No way could she face eating now—the food would make her sick. But she would have a drink. She flung open the fridge door and pulled out the bottle of champagne Slade had left to cool.

'Nice brand,' she said aloud, studying the label. 'I'll give you credit for one thing, cowboy—you're no miser when it comes to buying fine wines. Or was it simply the only one in the shop?' She carried the bottle through to the living-room, resentment still smouldering like embers within her as she irritably kicked off her high-heeled shoes and padded barefoot to the drinks cabinet. 'Something special to celebrate a special moment,' she said softly, running her eyes over the selection of bottles. Then she gave a little chuckle as she spotted what she was looking for. 'Brandy and champagne—what could be more appropriate? After all, it's not every day you throw away your heart and your job in one fell swoop.' She twisted the cork of the champagne bottle free without spilling a drop of the sparkling liquid, and added a generous quantity to the measure of brandy already in the glass. Then she held up the glass, tilting her head back as she addressed the empty room.

'This is a toast,' she said loftily. 'To Ross Stuart and Christine Bell-Reilly. May they meet up in some kind of afterlife and plague hell out of each other the way they've plagued me on earth.' She lifted the glass to her lips and took a hefty swallow, coughing as the champagne bubbles hit her throat. She grabbed both bottles by the neck and carried them along with her glass to the armchair before the fire, placing them carefully on the floor before throwing herself into the cushions, taking another swig on the way.

'So,' she said brightly, looking deep into the flickering flames, 'tell me my future, fire—what's it to be? Street sweeper perhaps? Or will some far-sighted editor spot the unmistakable brilliance in me and sign me up on the spot? Because I can tell you one thing, old buddy—I won't write a single word about that man now—not for anybody.' She paused to add more champagne to the glass. 'And you know something else? All of a sudden I don't care. I don't care what old Mother Reilly does—and I don't care what he does either. As far as I'm concerned, they're both out of my life forever, and good riddance to both of them. I hope I never have to see either of them again.'

She sat there in the big old chair for a long time, just watching the fire and mixing the champagne and brandy. Finally the combination proved too much for her and she gazed woozily about the room, wondering why it had suddenly started to move of its own volition.

'Guess I must be drunk,' she muttered dopily, focusing with difficulty on the half-empty bottle. 'Well, that's all to the good. I hope I have a crashing hangover tomorrow—then I won't be able to think about him.' She laid the glass down on the hearth and snuggled sleepily into the armchair.

'Never did like Slade Keller anyway,' she murmured, as sleep overcame her. 'But I wish I could have said goodbye to Ross.'

CHAPTER NINE

LEIGH was dragged sickeningly back to reality some time later, when the smell of smoke, thick and acrid in the air, assaulted her dreams.

'What on earth?' She leapt to her feet, still dazed and groggy from the alcohol she had sunk, coughing hard as the smoke hit her lungs. Acting more by instinct than good sense, she flung open the outside door, standing for a second to breathe in the clean cold night air, then dived back inside. The smoke was coming through the open archway leading to the kitchen and she forced herself to head in that direction, though her eyes were beginning to stream and breathing was becoming all but impossible.

'Dear God!' The exclamation was ripped from her as she spotted the smoke pouring out of the cooker. A quick glance at the wall told her what had happened—she had flicked the wrong switch earlier, turning off, not the cooker as she had intended, but the coffee percolator which was plugged in to the other side of the double socket. Now the Steak Wellington was burnt to a cinder, and threatening to turn the place into a thick black cloud of smoke. She grabbed a kitchen towel from the table and held it under the tap, then swathed the wet cloth about her face. Still coughing, she picked up a second towel and was about to make a lunge for the oven door when another thought struck her and she recoiled in horror. The oven held not only the steaks—but also a dish of potatoes roasting in oil—if she opened the door now, she risked being met by a sheet of flame.

'Sweet Lord help me,' she prayed aloud. 'I don't know what to do.'

'Leigh, get away from there!' The voice ripped through her fuddled brain as she bent towards the oven door and she looked up to see Ross charging into the kitchen. Before she could speak he grabbed her arm and flung her bodily away from the cooker. Caught completely off balance, she lost her footing and slammed into the side of the archway. With a tiny whimper, she fainted clean away, sinking to the floor as the swirling darkness enveloped her brain. Her last thought was that she hadn't warned Ross about the oil, but the words died on her lips as consciousness fled.

When she came to she was lying on the ground some distance from the cottage, her head on a folded-up sweater, her body covered by a heavy sheepskin jacket. She struggled to sit up, only to be gently pushed down again.

'Lie easy, sweetheart,' Ross's voice murmured softly in her ear. 'Everything's OK—the fire's out, and the cottage is safe apart from a little smoke damage.'

'Ross,' she croaked through a raw, painful throat, 'there was hot oil in the cooker.'

She caught the gleam of his white teeth as he grinned in the gloom. 'I know. I found that out pretty quick!'

'Were you hurt?'

He shook his head. 'Burned my hand a touch. Nothing serious. I'm more worried about you right now—you got a good lungful of that smoke and you fell pretty hard when I pushed you out of the way. Did I hurt you, honey?'

The concern in his voice triggered the tears and there was nothing she could do to stop them as they trickled down her face, streaking the smoke and grime on her skin.

'No,' she sobbed. 'You didn't hurt me, I just fell awkwardly. I don't know why I'm crying Ross, I...'

'Hush, baby.' Gently he stroked the hair away from her filthy face. 'It's just the effects of the shock on top of everything else. Let the tears come—they're good for you.' He took her in his arms then and she cried freely, feeling as though the river would never cease.

'How did you know?' she managed to stammer out at last, the effort of talking still hurting her throat.

'About the fire? I was walking outside—couldn't face going to bed somehow, knew I'd never sleep. I smelt the smoke.' His eyes narrowed as he held her close, feeling the trembling in her limbs. 'When I saw you bending over that stove about to open the oven door, I just freaked. Leigh, you could have been so badly burned.'

'But you did it,' she murmured against his shoulder. 'You tackled the fire.'

'I knew what I was doing,' he said grimly. 'The same thing happened once on the ranch—but we were a long way from any fire station, so my father had seen to it that we could all tackle blazes.'

'God, the place must be in such a mess,' she groaned. 'Poor Jack—his beautiful cottage.'

'If I know Jack as well as I think I do, he'll be mighty glad it's just things and not people that have been damaged. He'd have been devastated if anything had happened to you. Anyway, I've called him. He's on his way over with a doctor.'

'I don't need a doctor.'

'In a pig's eye you don't.' He held her away for a moment, gazing searchingly into her eyes. 'Why did it take so long for you to notice the smoke? It must have been pretty strong.'

She looked shamefaced. 'I was dead to the world,' she admitted. 'Bombed out on champagne and brandy—I'm surprised anything woke me at all.'

'Champagne and brandy?' He shook his head in amazement. 'I'll get to the bottom of that one later. But right now I want to get you indoors. You're shivering.'

'I don't want to go back into the cottage,' she clutched his arm convulsively, 'I'm not ready to see it yet.'

'Hey, lady, what do you take me for? Just some big dumb cowboy?' His smile took the sting from his words. 'We're going back to my place. Just you hang on to me.'

'I can walk by myself,' she protested, but even as she struggled to get to her feet, she felt her legs give way beneath her and he scooped her easily into his arms.

'Look, honey, you can be as independent as you like tomorrow. But right now, just give in and lean a little.'

She slid her arms about his neck with a grateful sigh. 'OK.'

He carried her easily down the path to his cottage and upstairs to his room, laying her gently on the bed.

'You look a mess,' he said tenderly.

'So do you.' She tried to laugh but it turned into a racking cough.

'Lie still. I'll be back in a moment.'

She lay back against the pillows, trying to come to terms with all that had happened. A few hours ago she had been yelling like a demented banshee at the man, now here she was lying on his bed. Physically she felt a wreck—her chest felt tight and sore, her throat was raw, her eyes still smarting from the smoke. But deep inside there was a strange warmth, and it didn't take much guessing to know who was responsible for that. Ross had been so sweet—so kind and compassionate. He could have been angry—after all, the fire had been the result of her own stupidity—instead he had taken care of her. Because he's a good man, she told herself wonderingly. Underneath the arrogance and the pride, he's a fine person—you should have known he would never turn away from a person in need. But why should he ever regard you as a friend? As far as he's concerned, you've only ever wanted something from him—never the man for himself.

'But that's not true,' she murmured aloud. 'It never was.'

'What did you say?' Ross came back into the room and sat down on the bed beside her. 'Budge up a little.'

Obediently she moved along, her eyes soft as she watched him. For the first time she really did feel as if she was back with Ross again—he wasn't putting on any kind of act now, but simply being himself, and the knowledge of it melted her very bones.

'I didn't really say anything,' she said quietly. 'I was just talking to myself. What are you doing?'

'Cleaning you up a little.' He gently wiped her face with a damp flannel. 'You don't want to see the doc with a dirty face, do you?'

She closed her eyes as the damp cloth moved carefully over her skin. Then Ross gave a sharp exclamation and her eyes flew open. 'What is it?'

'You've got a nasty bruise here on your temple.' He frowned, peering closely at the discoloured skin. 'I thought it was dirt at first, but it's not.' He turned slightly to look into her eyes and the breath caught in her throat. His face was less than a couple of inches from her own—it would be so easy to bridge the gap and press her lips to his—to slide her arms about his neck and feel his body against her own.

For a long moment neither of them moved, then she licked her dry lips and forced words past a strangely constricted throat.

'That must have happened when I fell,' she said huskily.

'Hell's bells—then I did that to you.' It was the stricken look in his eyes that did it—she just couldn't bear to see him that way, and without even thinking about it she flung her arms about him, pulling his head down on to her shoulder. 'Only to save me from something much worse! I could have been badly burned, if you hadn't pushed me out of the way.'

His arms tightened about her and she felt a wild surge of exhilaration. After all this time, to be held this way by him, it just didn't seem possible. The fevered caresses in the hotel room hadn't counted, they had been born of anger, but this was a healing moment—an infinitely precious embrace.

'Ross, are you up there?'

Jack's voice broke the moment, and she pulled reluctantly away, feeling instantly bereft as he released her. But the look in his eyes told her more than words ever could and she lay back against the pillows, feeling happier than she had been in a very long time.

'We're in here.' Ross stood up to greet Jack and the doctor, a kindly-faced, grey-haired man carrying a medical bag. Jack took one look at Leigh lying on the bed and hurried to her side.

'My God, Leigh, are you OK? When Ross phoned I imagined all sorts of horrors—you could have been killed in there!'

She grinned, putting a hand on his arm to stop the flow of anxious words.

'I'm fine,' she said. 'Honestly. Just a little smoky, that's all. But how's the cottage? Is it badly damaged?'

Jack ran a harassed hand through his hair, leaving it standing on end. 'To hell with the cottage,' he ground out. 'There's nothing there that can't be replaced. It's you and Ross I'm worried about.'

'I've already told you, I'm fine—thanks to Ross.' Her eyes strayed to the tall figure standing by the window.

'Well, young lady, how about letting me have a look at you anyway.' The doctor gently shooed Jack from the bedside and took his place. 'And if you two gentlemen would be good enough to scarper and give us a little privacy?'

Jack and Ross took the hint and ambled out of the room, Ross turning at the last moment to wink at Leigh. She smiled back, suddenly feeling ridiculously happy.

'I must say, you don't look too bad,' the doctor said drily, not missing the light in her eyes. 'But I'll give you the once-over just in case. Did you breathe in a lot of smoke?'

Fifteen minutes later the doctor joined Jack and Ross downstairs in the living-room.

'She's fine,' he grinned broadly as both men jumped to their feet, obviously full of questions.

'She's a very healthy young woman, fortunately. A couple of days of rest and comfort and she'll be as good as new—especially if she gets some of the island's good clean air into her lungs. I was going to give her a sedative, but she told me she'd been drinking earlier this evening.' He smiled. 'The alcohol still in her system will probably help her sleep anyway.'

'What about shock?' Ross handed a tumbler of whisky to the doctor.

'Thanks. I can't see any immediate signs of shock, though of course these things can be delayed. As I say, make sure she stays fairly quiet for a couple of days—and give me a call if there are any problems. Now then,' he fixed Ross with a determined look, 'it's your turn. I want to examine you too.'

'There's no need.' Ross waved a dismissive hand, and Jack chuckled.

'You might as well just give in,' he said. 'I've known the doc for years—he doesn't let prospective patients off the hook that easily.'

'Quite right.' The grey-haired man polished off the whisky in a couple of swallows and set the tumbler down. 'So be a good fellow and get your shirt off.'

Ross submitted to the examination with a few good-natured grumbles, then managed to usher the two men out, after promising faithfully to look after Leigh and to call Jack if she needed anything.

'And tell her not to worry about the cottage. I'll round up a few of the women from the village—they'll have it looking good as new in no time.'

'I'll do that,' Ross said patiently, having already assured Jack on the same point at least five times. 'Now go, both of you, otherwise you won't get any sleep at all tonight.'

'Never mind that, but just make sure Leigh knows...'

'I think Mr Stuart knows exactly what to do, Jack.' The doctor gently pushed him to the door, looking back at Ross with an understanding grin. 'Now move, before I decide to give you an examination too, just for the hell of it.'

'OK, OK!' Jack held up his hands in surrender. 'For someone who's supposed to minister to sick people, you can be a real old grouch sometimes, you know that?'

Ross stood watching as the two men walked to the car, then groaned as Jack suddenly jumped out of the passenger seat again. What other instructions could he possibly be about to make now?

'I've been meaning to give you these for a couple of days now.' Jack thrust a plastic carrier bag into his hand. 'I won't make any comment about them—make up your own mind.' And before Ross could say a single word, he loped off back to the car. Ross waved the car away, then turned back to the cottage with a rueful grin. Jack was a fine man and a good friend—but faced with the possibility of Leigh being hurt, he had turned as fussy as an old mother hen. Still, it was nice to meet someone who could be so open about their feelings—he was sick to the heart of those who would smile to his face and say one thing, while plotting something entirely different behind his back. Just the way Leigh had done. The thought darkened his eyes—even now the memory of her betrayal rankled—no, it did a lot more than that. If he was to be honest with himself—it had cut him straight to the heart. Back in those terrific carefree days on the island, he had found himself on the verge of falling in love with the beautiful golden-haired girl. He had taken her entirely at face value for the sweet, generous, loving creature she had seemed to be—he had even started to weave dreams for the future in which she played the central role. She would have been a breath of fresh air in his world—and he had really needed the undemanding, straightforward loving she seemed to be offering. Discovering she was really just like all the rest—out for what she could get from him—had been almost more than he could take.

Caught up in his own dark thoughts he switched off the living-room lights and made his way upstairs, intending to sleep in the spare room. He had automatically carried Leigh to his own bed because it was the more comfortable of the two, but the smaller room would suit him fine for one night. But as he reached Leigh's door, something stopped him and he reached for the handle without consciously realising what he was doing. He had expected to find her tucked up beneath the covers—instead she was lying on top of the quilt, still fully clothed. She must have gone out like a light—little wonder considering the amount of alcohol she had sunk earlier. He frowned at the thought—just what the hell had all that been about, anyway? The Leigh he remembered had never been much of a drinker—she had taken a glass or two of wine, but that was about it. And he was somehow sure she hadn't turned to the bottle in the intervening years—her skin was too clear, her eyes too bright for that. He knew all the tell-tale signs—had seen all too many of his friends and colleagues turning to alcohol and paying the price for it. So why tonight? Why had she turned to drink—and to such a lethal combination? It was the kind of thing someone would do if they were in real pain and had been pushed beyond the limits of their endurance. Had he done that to her?

He sat down on the edge of the bed, his eyes never leaving her face. She looked so vulnerable in sleep—the wary, watchful look he had grown accustomed to had disappeared, leaving only peace. He could understand the lure of alcohol as a means of dulling the senses—Lord knew he'd been tempted along the same route five years before when he had first left the island, angry, bitter and disillusioned. In a way he had been in a worse state then than when he had returned from Vietnam—for who in this day and age could ever go off to war with any illusions of glory? The world he'd found there had been dirty and sickening—but it hadn't been much different from his expectations. But in Leigh he had truly believed he'd found his dream—she was the true golden girl, full of life, laughter and love, and it had seemed back then that she was willing to give it all to him. Oh, yes, he could have gone to the booze on leaving her—instead, he had buried himself in work, churning out one film after another, for a while not even bothering about the quality of his work. Much the same could be said for the women who had filled his bed over that crazy time—they had been warm and willing, and appeared from nowhere in plentiful supply—but he would be hard pushed now even to remember their names. After a while he had got himself together again—but he'd never been able to free himself completely of the memory of the girl on the enchanted island. A couple of years back he had decided to visit Britain, with the express intention of finding her—a trip that was meant to satisfy the tiny, barely acknowledged part of him that had always hoped he would be proved wrong about Leigh—that he would somehow discover against all the odds that she really was the girl he'd fallen for, and not a devious schemer. Then, a matter of days before he was due to fly out, he had seen the gossip column in the magazine—seeing her name on the by-line had given him an undeniable jolt of excitement—but reading the column with its snide innuendoes had sickened him to the stomach. He had cancelled the trip, vowing he would never allow himself to think of her again. Only somehow it just hadn't worked out that way. This trip had been a final bid to lay the ghost to rest—and in the most dramatic way. He had set out with the sole intention of wreaking revenge—of getting rid of the bitterness he had carried for so long by somehow hurting her, humiliating her, in just the way she'd hurt him.

Tonight she had sworn that column hadn't been her work and he had thrown her words back in her face, refusing to believe her. Well, judging by the amount of alcohol she had taken afterwards, he had certainly succeeded in hurting her—but, it seemed, not in the way he had expected. Having believed for so long she didn't have a heart, he had taken a stab at her professional pride—but her reaction had been way too extreme—could she really have been telling the truth after all? But even if that was the case—why should his refusal to believe her have hurt her so very deeply?

As he watched her sleep, Leigh gave a tiny shiver and he scowled at his own thoughtlessness. Well done, big-shot, he murmured under his breath—just leave the poor kid to freeze to death while you try to sort out your own crazy mixed-up head. And just try explaining that one to Jack! He moved quietly through to the other bedroom and pulled the quilt from the bed. He wasn't likely to get much sleep tonight anyway, so she might as well have the benefit of the cover. Returning to her room, he tucked the quilt carefully about her, smiling as she murmured in her sleep. He would give a lot to know what she was dreaming about right now.

He pulled a hard-backed chair over from the wall and set it down at the bedside, then noticed the carrier bag Jack had given him lying on the floor.

He picked it up, a frown crossing his features as he saw what was inside—half a dozen copies of the *She Speaks* magazine. Now just what was Jack trying to tell him with those? As Leigh slumbered on, unaware, he began to flick through the glossy pages, glancing up occasionally towards the sleeping figure in the bed as the words unfolded themselves before his eyes. And when she finally stirred in the morning, his face was the first thing she saw.

CHAPTER TEN

'GOOD morning.' Sleepily she stretched her arms above her head. 'Have you been there all night?'

'Sure feels like it.' Wearily he rubbed his neck, trying to get rid of the kinks.

'But why?'

He grinned. 'Guess you could say the view was too good to leave.'

She looked down at herself, puzzled, only to realise her split skirt had misbehaved during the night and was now rucked up behind her, leaving both long legs uncovered.

'Ross! You could have thrown a blanket over me.'

'I did.' He nodded towards the quilt lying crumpled at her side. 'You kept kicking it off. I gave up in the end—decided you must be warm enough without it.'

And getting hotter by the second, she thought dazedly, feeling a strange tremor as his eyes ran unhurriedly over her body.

'I must get up,' she said, suddenly needing to escape his eyes.

'You must not.' He stood up and gently but firmly pushed her back when she tried to swing her legs to the floor.

'But I have to get back to the cottage—clear it up for Jack.'

'Jack's got that well in hand—and the doc left explicit instructions that you were to spend the day doing a whole lot of nothing. Understand?'

'But the whole thing was my fault! I can't leave all the messy work to someone else.' She pushed against his restraining hands, but it had the same effect as shoving a brick wall.

'Lord, but you're a stubborn woman! Look, if you put so much as one toe over the doorstep of that cottage, Jack will send you packing—and I'll be there to pick you up and carry you back here. Now do you understand?'

The thought of being carried anywhere in those powerful arms was almost enough to make her accept the challenge, but at the last she subsided against the pillows, a mutinous look in her eyes. 'I suppose so,' she grumbled. 'But you're a pair of bullies. You can't really expect me to stay in bed all day.'

'You may get up to have a bath—get some of that disgusting smoke out of your skin and hair,' he conceded. 'And if you're very good, I might even take you for a walk later. But that's it.'

'Didn't the doctor give you any orders? You were in the smoke too.'

He grinned, his eyes creasing at the corners. 'Maybe he did. But I'm bigger than he is. Now just lie still. I'll run a bath for you, then bring breakfast up here.'

'Look, that's really not . . .'

'Woman, will you do as you're told for once in your life!' Ignoring her protests, he picked up the discarded quilt and tucked it firmly about her legs. 'And make the most of it. It's not every day the world-famous Slade Keller serves breakfast in bed, you know.'

His words were self-mocking, but they slammed into her with the force of a boxer's punch. So they were back to that again—after all that had happened in the past few hours, she had almost managed to forget that other side of him—had simply revelled in the undiluted joy of being with Ross again. But that was crazy—nothing more than a foolish dream.

She heard the sounds of taps being turned on and water rushing into the bath and lay back, fighting the sudden sting of tears. There was no point in crying—just because a fantasy had been allowed to live again for a few short hours—just because he had held her in his arms all over again—nothing had really changed. No kindly angel had descended to wave a magic wand and wipe away his other life—and all the old misunderstandings still existed, they had simply been set aside for a little while, like a truce in the middle of a war.

When he came back to tell her the bath was ready, she thanked him without meeting his eyes and padded past him on bare feet to the bathroom, locking the door firmly behind her. She spent a long time in the bath, letting the warm water ease the tension from her bones, shampooing her hair several times over to get rid of the smell of smoke still lingering. Just a shame she couldn't wash him out as easily, she thought ruefully—but it seemed he was destined to play a part in her life, and always a destructive part at that. So he was being sweet to her right now—that would doubtless change soon enough. She would be a fool to think otherwise.

Well, she had done her best, she told herself, reaching for the shower spray to rinse her hair. She had gone along with the crazy scheme, done all that Bell-Reilly had demanded of her. But in the end she had failed—no way could she bring herself to write the article, even though she had more than enough material. But she could never hope to achieve the kind of objectivity she prided herself on—in fact she had been a fool ever to think she could. There just wasn't a remote chance of standing back from this one and looking at it through a stranger's eyes. In any case, when it came right down to it, she found she didn't want to—didn't want to deliver the man up in a nicely typed bundle of paper—didn't want to spread out his life story for thousands of anonymous eyes to read. The last few days she shared with him had been all she would ever have—she just couldn't let anyone else in on that. In a little while she would tell him—not that it would make any difference of course. No matter how nice he was being to her right now, she knew his prejudice against her ran too deep for her to change his mind now. But it was the only thing she could give him—since he would never accept her love.

She stepped out of the bath and wrapped a towel around herself, then wound another round her wet hair. Tentatively she opened the door and listened for a moment. Sounds from downstairs reassured her he was still in the kitchen and she padded quickly across the hall, intending to be back in bed before he returned. The dress she had been wearing was too grubby and smoke-stained to put on again, but she spotted one of Ross's tartan shirts lying on the chair. If he was going to be so insistent about her staying in bed, he would just have to supply the bedwear.

She towelled her hair as dry as she could get it, using a comb from the dresser to get rid of the tangles. Then she dropped the towel on the floor and slid her arms into the shirt. The material was soft and well worn and she hugged it to her, pretending for just a second that his arms were round her again. His smell, subtle yet definitely masculine, clung to the shirt, making it easy to imagine he really was there.

'Hey, that looks a lot better on you than on me!' The sound of his laughing voice at the door made her jump guiltily and she swung round to face him.

'I hope you don't mind,' she said breathlessly, wondering just how long he had been standing there. 'My dress is dirty.'

'Of course I don't mind,' he said easily, setting down the tray he carried on the table beside the bed. 'I had intended to go back to your place to get some fresh clothes for you, but I'll leave that till later. You look just great in that shirt—even if it is a little on the generous side.'

She glanced downwards, chuckling at the sight of the sleeves hanging below her hands, the hemline almost reaching her knees.

'Don't you know it's all the rage for women to wear men's clothes?' she said loftily.

'Never did pay much heed to fashion, ma'am.' He deliberately deepened his American drawl. 'I'm just a farm boy, remember? Where I grew up there was a very definite line between the sexes.'

She nodded, a teasing glint in her eyes. 'Where the men were men and the women were...'

'Glad of it.' He finished the sentence and the breath blocked in his throat as he took a step towards her. 'But no one could ever mistake you for anything other than a beautiful woman no matter what you were wearing.' He was so close now she could see the amber flecks in his tawny eyes, could feel the warmth of his breath whispering over her skin.

'Ross, I...'

'Hush, moonlight lady,' he murmured, and the sound of the old endearment sent a rush of heat to her skin. She closed her eyes, wondering wildly if the giddiness clouding her brain was simply an after-effect of the night before. Then his lips gently brushed hers, and her knees nearly gave way beneath her. She tried to speak, but no words came, and without even realising what she was doing, she found herself kissing him back, her lips parting at the soft insistence of his probing tongue. His arms closed about her, pulling her tight against his hard body, and she strained in his embrace, aching to be closer, closer still, till there was no longer any kind of space between them. He nibbled at the fullness of her lower lip, and any resistance she might have felt took wing and fled—how could she resist something she had been longing for with every fibre of her being? When he lifted his head at last, the cloudy, unfocused look in his eyes reflected her own.

It was only by a supreme effort that she managed to pull back from him, loosening his embrace. 'Ross, please,' she said breathlessly. 'We have to talk.'

For a second she thought he was about to ignore her words, and knew she would never have the strength or the will to resist if his lips touched hers again, but at last he nodded.

'You're right,' he said. 'But pour us both a coffee first—I've got a feeling we might need it.'

Regretfully she stepped away from him—who knew, that might have been the last embrace they would ever share—but she couldn't let it go any further without making at least one last ditch attempt at setting things straight between them.

She poured the coffee, smiling as she noticed the trembling of her hand. Would she ever be able to see this man and not tremble?

'I'm not even sure where to start,' she said shakily, sitting down on the bed and tucking her long legs under her. 'Even though I've wished for this opportunity a thousand times.'

'You have?' His eyes regarded her thoughtfully. 'Why?'

'That's not important right now.' Because it would tell you far too much about how I feel—how I've always felt for you, she added silently. 'I've decided not to write the article about you.' She held up one hand as he began to speak. 'No, please let me have my say. This may be the only chance I ever get.' She smiled wistfully, letting her eyes drink in the sight of the man sitting opposite. 'There are moments in everyone's lives when they're forced to make choices. In your case I imagine you have to make a choice whenever you're offered a new film—is it a good one, is it worth doing, is this a character you really want to portray?' She paused as he nodded in agreement. 'But in the early days perhaps you didn't have so much say in the matter—perhaps you had to do things you'd rather not have done. When we first met, I was just a cub reporter—a novice, covering all the flower shows and golden weddings. I didn't have any choices to make then, I simply did whatever the boss told me. Then he decided to send me here—to Arran. I'd never even heard of it, though it was part of our patch. My editor told me it was a kind of a challenge—that if I was ever to call myself a real reporter, I'd first have to prove I could find news anywhere.' She smiled, remembering how disgusted she had been with the assignment. 'I felt at first that I'd been given a raw deal—but I was determined not to fail, even though I hadn't a clue where to start. Then, I heard two women talking in a café.' She paused, looking a little sheepish. 'Yes, I know, that's probably just the sort of thing you deplore most, eavesdropping on other people's conversations. Anyway—they were talking about you. I just couldn't believe it—Slade Keller, the film star, here on a tiny island? It seemed a totally off-the-wall idea. But if it was true...'

'It would be the biggest break ever likely to come your way.' He cut into her words, nodding slowly. 'Just like a struggling actor suddenly finding a Broadway producer sitting on his front porch.'

'Exactly!' Her eyes lit up in delight at his words. Could she really be reaching him at last? 'But the whole world knew Slade Keller was impossible to pin down to an interview. You were notorious!' She paused, looking suddenly stricken. 'Now I understand why you hated journalists so much—but I'd never read the piece done after Vietnam. If I had...'

'Never mind that now. Go on with your own story.' He smiled, understanding the distress in her eyes.

'Well,' she continued slowly, 'that's the reason I couldn't come clean with you when we first met. I was afraid I'd lose you before I'd even begun.'

'And you wouldn't have landed your scoop.'

She nodded. 'That's right. But that was only important in the beginning.'

His eyes narrowed. 'What do you mean? Surely to a reporter, that was the only important thing.'

'Not after I'd started to get to know you.' Her cheeks coloured faintly, as she realised she was getting into dangerous territory. 'I found out very quickly I didn't have all the right instincts—not enough of the shark in me I suppose.' She laughed self-consciously, not quite meeting his eyes. 'What I'm trying to say is that we became friends—I grew—fond—of you. I could no longer see you as just a story—you were a real person to me.'

'Thanks for the compliment,' he cut in drily.

'Please! Don't you see—as a film star you were fair game. But to me you were Ross Stuart—a very different kettle of fish.'

'Can't say I can recall ever being described quite that way before,' he drawled, highly amused by the expression. 'But why didn't you just own up then?'

She glanced down at her untouched cup of coffee. 'I should have. But I was afraid.'

'Of losing the story?'

'No, dammit! Of losing you!' She bit her lip, appalled at what she had just revealed. She had never intended to admit so much.

'Go on,' he said softly, his eyes never leaving her face.

'Well,' it was hard to know how to continue without getting into a deeper mess than ever, 'I kept up the pretence as long as I could because I . . .' she paused, feeling herself turn scarlet before his very eyes, 'because I wanted to hang on to what we had for as long as I possibly could.' The words came out in a rush. 'Can you understand that? I knew all along it was an impossible situation—for one thing I was a member of a profession you hated—and if that wasn't bad enough, you came from an entirely different world. Things could never have worked out between us. I knew even then that I'd have to lose you when it was time for you to go back to the States—but I just wanted to—to hold on, I guess.'

'Would you have let me go without telling me the truth?' he asked quietly.

She gave him a sad little smile. 'That's the awful irony of the whole thing. Do you remember that last morning?' He nodded slowly and she swallowed hard against the rising lump in her throat. It was still hard to think of that terrible day. 'I don't suppose you'll believe me now, but I had it all planned—I was going to tell you that day. I was going to ask you to go for a walk with me, and I was going to tell you everything.'

'Why then?'

She shrugged helplessly. 'Because I'd had enough of all the secrecy. I wanted things to be open and honest between us.' She glanced up at him, her eyes faintly accusing. 'Don't forget, you'd been lying to me too—you'd never admitted your real identity.'

'Maybe because I needed to forget it for a little while.'

She nodded. 'That's what I always assumed. Anyway, things didn't work out the way I'd planned. You found my notebook and Press card—and you know the rest for yourself.'

He leaned forward, his eyes darkening. 'Was it a good story?'

She gave him a puzzled look. 'What story?'

'The one you wrote about me, of course. I never saw it. Did it give you the break you'd hoped for?'

For a second she felt an insane desire to laugh. Had he really believed all these years that she had gone ahead with the article—after all that had happened between them?

'Dear heaven, Ross, just what do you take me for?' she cried wildly. 'Haven't you understood a single word I've said? I gave up the idea of writing that story very soon after meeting you.'

She watched in fascination as the colour drained from his face. 'Is that really the truth?' he said hoarsely. 'You could easily have written something—you knew enough about me by that time.'

She threw up her hands in frustration. 'Dammit, that wasn't the point! It was *because* I knew you, you block-headed idiot!'

'But all these years—I've believed you did write it.'

'Didn't you stop to wonder why I hadn't written more than a couple of sentences about you in my notebook—didn't you ever wonder why the article hadn't ever landed on your lap? Surely you have a clippings service—most actors do.'

'I've made it a policy never to read anything about myself ever since the Vietnam piece,' he said. 'My agent handles all that—but he knows never to pass anything on to me.'

A sudden thought struck her and she groaned. 'So when you saw that awful gossip column you assumed I'd simply gone from bad to worse—you thought you'd been right about me all along.'

The merest shadow of a smile touched his lips. 'I guess you could say that.'

She gave a hollow laugh. 'Then that's the worst irony of them all. You see, it's partly because of you that I decided I'd never write that type of story—yes, I did do the column for a few months, but not the one you read. And the things I included in it were mere snippets of trivia, nothing that could have hurt anyone.' Her eyes held his. 'I'd seen at first hand the effect that kind of intrusive journalism could have—I didn't know then about the Vietnam story of course, but it was easy to see you'd had a bad experience with the Press—I swore I'd never deliberately make anyone else feel that way. Everything I've ever written has had a purpose and a meaning to it—yes, I've exposed people in print, but never just for the hell of it, never to satisfy the readers' base instincts alone.'

'I know that.' His softly spoken words cut into her monologue and she froze.

'What did you say?'

'You heard me.' He leaned over and took her hand in his own, studying her long slender fingers as he considered his words. 'Last night, just before he left the cottage, Jack gave me a whole bundle of *She Speaks* magazines—he's obviously a big fan of yours, must have been saving the back copies for years. Anyway, while you slept, I did a lot of reading—and what I read kind of opened my eyes.' Those same eyes gazed deep into her own, and for a long moment she felt as though her heart had ceased to beat. 'You're a hell of a writer, Leigh Daniels—and judging by the kind of things you've been courageous enough to write about, you're a hell of a person too. It must have taken real guts to track down some of that information—it doesn't lie around on coffee-tables waiting to be picked up.'

'You've read my work?' She barely heard the compliments—was simply stunned by the first revelation. 'You really sat there all night and read things I'd written? But why?'

'Why?' His eyebrows shot upwards, disappearing beneath the heavy lock of hair falling over his forehead. 'Because it was important to me, you silly girl. And you know what? I learned more about you in just a few hours than I've known in five years.' Still holding her hand, he slowly got to his feet and moved over to sit beside her on the bed.

'Like what exactly?' His sudden closeness was all but robbing her of the power to breathe.

He tilted his head back, considering the question. 'That you're warm and compassionate—that shone through in the piece you did on the little mentally handicapped girl—that you're a fighter—that was clear in the piece you'd done on local government bungling; I bet quite a few people had cause to be grateful to you for that one. But most of all, your integrity shone through every single piece I read, Leigh Daniels—and since you pour your very heart into what you write, there can be no doubting your sincerity too. If you had written the article about me, I know it would have been fair and generous, even after the despicable way I treated you.'

'Despicable?' She had to repeat the word simply to make sure she had heard him correctly. 'But haven't you always thought...'

'It was the other way round?' He finished the question for her. 'I've been a fool, Leigh—a damn crazy fool. I never stopped long enough for you to explain anything to me—I was so all-fired sure I'd been duped all over again, I was blind to everything else. I over-reacted—went way over the top, but I never stopped long enough to wonder why. Now I have.'

'And?' she whispered the word, almost afraid to believe what she was seeing in his eyes.

'And I know I went crazy back then because I'd fallen in love with you. That's why your apparent betrayal was so hard to take.'

'Oh, God, Ross.' She couldn't stand the distance between them any longer, just had to be touching him. She lifted a hand to his face and he caught it, pressing it to his lips.

'If I hadn't been so mad about you, none of it would have mattered as much as it did,' he groaned. 'I'd have been angry, sure—but not devastated. But the whole thing damn near ripped me apart—I didn't ever think I'd get the pieces together again.' His arms went about her and she leaned against him, all but overwhelmed by the force of her feelings. There was jubilation there deep inside—but it was mixed in with a terrible sadness, she realised sorrowfully. He really had loved her once—he had told her so. But that was in the past—he hadn't said a word about how he felt for her right now, and that in itself told her everything she had to know. He was obviously still fond of her—that showed in the way he was treating her now—maybe in a physical sense she could still turn him on. But he had put back the pieces without her help—or so he had hinted. Through a daze she felt his fingers stroking warmth into her skin, sliding beneath the tartan shirt to cup one naked breast. She should stop him—put an end to this right now before she had her own heart broken all over again. Only it felt so good—her hands found themselves tangling in his thick mane of hair, her lips parting of their own free will when his mouth sought them out.

'We shouldn't be doing this,' she rasped out. 'It doesn't solve any of our problems.'

'We'd never have had any problems in the first place if we'd only listened to our bodies, Leigh,' he murmured, swiftly freeing the buttons of her shirt. 'I told you when I first met you that our bodies knew exactly how to act with each other—it was only our ridiculous heads that got in the way.' He pushed the tartan material over her shoulders and gazed with darkening eyes on her nakedness. 'You smell so sweet, just like flowers in the morning.'

'It's bath oil.' She arched up to meet his seeking mouth against her breasts. 'We haven't talked enough, Ross—there's still so much to say.'

'You really want to have a conversation now?' He gazed into her unfocused eyes, letting his hand stroke a tantalisingly slow path along the silky skin of her thigh.

'I—I—oh Ross, don't stop doing that!'

'I didn't really intend to, honey.' A chuckle reverberated deep in his throat as she started tugging at his sweater, trying to haul it over his head. 'Easy, lady, I'd like to keep these ears—they're the only ones I've got.' He sat up slightly to help her and the sweater was flung heedlessly to the floor, followed seconds later by his jeans and boxer shorts.

Leigh opened her arms to him then, welcoming the weight of his hard muscled body lying along her own. All conscious thought had fled—all she knew was feeling, and the incredible sweetness of his touch. He moved restlessly over her, raining kisses on to her burning skin, the soft hairs of his moustache driving her nearly insane as they brushed over her. When his hand slipped between her legs, reaching the very heart of the fire coursing through her, she felt as if every bone in her body had melted clean away. The only reality lay in his roaming fingers and warm, searching lips—but if he didn't take her soon, she would explode through sheer monumental need.

'It's OK sweetheart,' the words whispered along her skin. 'I'm feeling just the same way. Next time we'll take it slow—but this one's been waiting way too long.' She felt her legs being pushed gently apart, then gasped aloud as he slid into her, his hard strength filling her, completing her, making her whole. She was instantly caught up in the rhythms of his movements and moved with him, driven only by need and the pent-up feelings bubbling deep inside. At the final moment when the pressure could be contained no longer, she cried his name aloud, pledging her love as the stars skyrocketed around her. She was only vaguely aware of Ross collapsing on top of her, utterly spent, but at last she was able to open her eyes and smile softly up at him.

'Hi.'

'Well, hi, yourself.' Grinning, he planted a kiss on her nose. 'Enjoy your trip?'

She chuckled. 'You could say that.'

'We shouldn't have done it, you know.'

The smile fled from her face. Was he really going to tell her he regretted making love? She would never be able to stand it.

'Why?' She could barely whisper the word.

'Because the doctor said you were supposed to stay quiet today—with absolutely no excitement.'

'Oh.' Her eyes lit up with relief and laughter. 'Well, that's OK, then.'

It was his turn to look bemused. 'You telling me you weren't excited back there?'

'Not a bit.' Then she subsided into giggles as his fingers started tickling her. 'No! Please! Don't do that—I can't stand it!'

'You want excitement, lady?' he growled deep in his throat. 'Well, you ain't seen nothin' yet.'

'What?' Her eyes flew open in amazement. 'You can't mean—not already—we've only just—oh, Ross, I can't believe this!'

'Believe it,' he said smugly, and his lips closed over hers, putting an end to all conversation.

It was a long time before either of them was in a fit enough state to talk again—caught up again and again in a storm that seemed determined not to abate. But finally they lay together on the verge of sleep, too exhausted to do any more than snuggle.

'Leigh?'

'Mmm?' His soft voice tugged her gently back to consciousness.

'You told me you loved me.'

She opened one eye, struggling to focus on his face, just a couple of inches from her own. 'I did?'

'You did.'

'Well, I guess I must, then.' And with a contented sigh she drifted off into sleep. It was only later that her words came back to her when she woke to an empty room and sat up abruptly. She had told him she loved him? How could she have been that crazy?

'Hi, sweetheart. Sleep well?' Wearing only a towel slung round his hips, Ross sauntered casually into the room, carrying a tray. 'You didn't make much inroad into that other meal, so I thought I'd try again,' he said, laying the tray on the table. 'What's wrong? Cat got your tongue?' He eyed her curiously, seeing the flush of pink in her cheeks, and the way she self-consciously tugged the quilt up to cover her nakedness. The sudden shyness after all that had passed between them surprised him, then he understood and smiled softly. 'Yes,' he said gently. 'You're right. You did say what you think you said.'

'Oh, hell.' She dropped her eyes to the coverlet. 'That's what I was afraid of.'

Tenderly he tipped her chin upwards. 'Afraid? Sweetheart, the words were only a bonus—your body spent the whole night telling me you loved me.'

'Well, you don't have to look so damn smug about it,' she muttered crossly, scowling as he gave a great shout of laughter.

'Smug? Is that what I'm looking?' He dropped down on to the bed beside her. 'Then we must have a language barrier here. What I'm feeling, lady, is happy—crazily, ridiculously happy—happier than I've felt in five long years if you want the truth of it.'

She stared at him, afraid to trust the glow that was beginning to warm the very centre of her being. 'Why?' she said cautiously.

'Why?' He screwed up his face, scratched his head in pretended puzzlement. 'Gee, that's a hard one. Guess it must be because I love you too. And I'd have told you so last night if you hadn't fallen asleep so fast.'

For a second she could do nothing more than gape at him open-mouthed, her eyes filled with a shimmering light. 'You love me? Honestly?'

'Yes, honestly! Is it so hard to believe?'

'After all that's happened between us?'

'Honey, none of it would have happened in the first place if we hadn't loved each other right from the start. I'd simply have lost my temper on discovering you were a reporter, threatened to sue your paper, and never bothered to give you another thought. Wouldn't have been the first time.' He grinned self-deprecatingly. 'Nor the last.'

'But what are we going to do about it?'

'Do?' He gazed at her quizzically. 'We'll do what we should have done in the first place—we'll stay together, of course—only next time we come up against any kind of problem, we'll work it through between us, instead of having one of us go storming off half-cocked.'

'Well, we've got a problem right now.' She said the words calmly enough, but inside her heart was thudding. Could he really be overlooking the obvious snags in their path? 'Like a problem of distance for one thing—if you haven't remembered, there's the little issue of you living in Tinseltown being a superstar, and me being a reporter in London. That's not exactly commuting distance, you know.'

He had been about to reach for a piece of toast, but her words stopped him midway. 'That's only a problem if we let it be one,' he said reasonably. 'What's to stop you living in the States? We do have newspapers out there, you know.'

She hesitated, wondering what effect her next words would have on him. 'But your world is so very different from mine, Ross,' she said softly. 'I'm not at all sure that I could exist in it. In fact—I'm afraid of it.'

He frowned. What crazy talk was this? Then his eyes cleared as he began to understand. 'Afraid of America?' he said carefully. 'Or afraid of your own image of the film world? There are good people and bad people there just as there are everywhere, Leigh—I won't kid you that it's a fairyland, but it's not so very bad.'

'But, it's such a—such a glamorous place.' She couldn't even look at him as she said the words.

To her surprise, he laughed softly. 'So that's what you're afraid of—that you won't be able to compete.'

'I don't want to compete, Ross!' She looked up at him with her heart in her eyes. 'I just don't want to give up everything I own and go out there only to find this is no more than a passing fancy for you, and that you're off every five minutes with the latest new starlet to hit the screen.'

He shook his head wonderingly, seeing the very real fears in her expressive eyes. 'Don't you know how gorgeous you are, Leigh?' he said softly. 'Don't you know you could stand up beside Hollywood's best and not be classed as second best? But in any case, your looks aren't important. Oh sure, your pretty face and your golden hair are a big bonus—I could look at them every day for the rest of my life and never cease marvelling at just how stunning you really are—but it's Leigh the person I'm in love with, not Leigh the face or Leigh the body. Hey—I'm a country boy, remember? I learned way back then that beauty's only ever skin-deep—my values were taught to me by people who knew the real beauty in life—and knew that it comes from within.' He paused. 'I may have come a long way since the ranch,' he said quietly, 'but I still carry those lessons with me.' He reached for her hand, gently squeezing her fingers in his own. 'Now—will you give it a try? Come to the States with me and see how things work out. If you hate it, we'll try something else.'

'But your career...'

'Ain't worth a can of beans if you're not there at my side to share it with me. And if you think that's just fancy talk—I can tell you that there hasn't been a single day these past five years when I haven't thought about you at least half a dozen times. You have to come with me, if only to save me from your own ghost!'

She chuckled softly and lifted his hand to her lips, softly kissing the hard skin of his fingers. 'If you put it like that, what can I say, but OK, cowboy?'

He gave a little whoop of delight and scooped her into his arms, the breakfast forgotten all over again. The rest of the world slid quietly away as their lips met in a promise that needed no words.

'Must be the moonlight,' Ross said decisively when he finally lifted his head. 'It's always addled my brain where you're concerned.'

Leigh cocked her head to the side, solemnly studying the ceiling. 'And there ain't even any moon,' she observed complacently.

'Exactly.'

Coming Next Month

#1215 FRIEND OR FOE Jenny Arden

Kira's late husband had given Glenn Mason guardianship over her stepdaughter, Heather—a fact Kira deeply resents. But his responsibility certainly doesn't give Glenn any right to interfere in her life—and sparks fly when he tries!

#1216 LOVERS TOUCH Penny Jordan

The only way Eleanor de Tressail can keep her promise to her grandfather to keep the estate in the family is a marriage of convenience to wealthy Joss Wycliffe. Only, for Eleanor, it is a case of love.

#1217 NOT WITHOUT LOVE Roberta Leigh

Julia's assignment is a challenge—to guard an engineer-inventor who has received death threats. Since Rees Denton refuses to have a bodyguard, Julia has to operate undercover as his personal assistant. But how can she watch over him at night?

#1218 WILD JUSTICE Joanna Mansell

Cassandra has enough problems coping with her overly possessive father, so she is furious when Jared Sinclair lures her to his isolated Scottish home for reasons entirely different from those he's given her. Surely it can't be just for revenge?

#1219 CHERISH THE FLAME Sandra Marton

Everyone's happy about Paige's forthcoming marriage to Alan Fowler—except his older brother, Quinn, who returns on the eve of the wedding. He tells Paige her father has been embezzling money from the Fowlers for years—and shocks her with the price for his silence!

#1220 THE DEVIL'S SHADOW Sally Wentworth

Her glamorous sister, Verity, spoiled Charlotte's early romance with Craig Bishop. Now, six years later, with Charlotte's dreams about to come true, Verity seems ready to do it again!

#1221 THE GATHERING DARKNESS Patricia Wilson

Nurse Julia Redford agrees to accompany her young patient Justine to her guardian's home in the Camargue. Julia has managed to cope with arrogant, overbearing Luc Marchal on her home ground, but once in France, Justine seems fine—and it's Luc who gives Julia problems!

#1222 BRAZILIAN FIRE Karen van der Zee

Chantal finds the sudden switch of life-styles from small-town America to the glamorous sophistication of Rio more than bewildering. She is even more puzzled by the cool, arrogant Enrico Chamberlain, who seems to hold her in such contempt!

Available in November wherever paperback books are sold, or through Harlequin Reader Service:

In the U.S.	In Canada
901 Fuhrmann Blvd.	P.O. Box 603
P.O. Box 1397	Fort Erie, Ontario
Buffalo, N.Y. 14240-1397	L2A 5X3

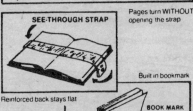

INDULGE A LITTLE SWEEPSTAKES

OFFICIAL RULES

SWEEPSTAKES RULES AND REGULATIONS. NO PURCHASE NECESSARY.

1. NO PURCHASE NECESSARY. To enter complete the official entry form and return with the invoice in the envelope provided. Or you may enter by printing your name, complete address and your daytime phone number on a 3 x 5 piece of paper. Include with your entry the hand printed words "Indulge A Little Sweepstakes." Mail your entry to: Indulge A Little Sweepstakes, P.O. Box 1397, Buffalo, NY 14269-1397. No mechanically reproduced entries accepted. Not responsible for late, lost, misdirected mail, or printing errors.

2. Three winners, one per month (Sept. 30, 1989, October 31, 1989 and November 30, 1989), will be selected in random drawings. All entries received prior to the drawing date will be eligible for that month's prize. This sweepstakes is under the supervision of MARDEN-KANE, INC. an independent judging organization whose decisions are final and binding. Winners will be notified by telephone and may be required to execute an affidavit of eligibility and release which must be returned within 14 days, or an alternate winner will be selected.

3. Prizes: 1st Grand Prize (1) a trip for two to Disneyworld in Orlando, Florida. Trip includes round trip air transportation, hotel accommodations for seven days and six nights, plus up to $700 expense money (ARV $3,500). 2nd Grand Prize (1) a seven-night Chandris Caribbean Cruise for two includes transportation from nearest major airport, accommodations, meals plus up to $1,000 in expense money (ARV $4,300). 3rd Grand Prize (1) a ten-day Hawaiian holiday for two includes round trip air transportation for two, hotel accommodations, sightseeing, plus up to $1,200 in spending money (ARV $7,700). All trips subject to availability and must be taken as outlined on the entry form.

4. Sweepstakes open to residents of the U.S. and Canada 18 years or older except employees and the families of Torstar Corp., its affiliates, subsidiaries and Marden-Kane, Inc. and all other agencies and persons connected with conducting this sweepstakes. All Federal, State and local laws and regulations apply. Void wherever prohibited or restricted by law. Taxes, if any are the sole responsibility of the prize winners. Canadian winners will be required to answer a skill testing question. Winners consent to the use of their name, photograph and/or likeness for publicity purposes without additional compensation.

5. For a list of prize winners, send a stamped, self-addressed envelope to Indulge A Little Sweepstakes Winners, P.O. Box 701, Sayreville, NJ 08871.

DL-SWPS

INDULGE A LITTLE SWEEPSTAKES

OFFICIAL RULES

SWEEPSTAKES RULES AND REGULATIONS. NO PURCHASE NECESSARY.

1. NO PURCHASE NECESSARY. To enter complete the official entry form and return with the invoice in the envelope provided. Or you may enter by printing your name, complete address and your daytime phone number on a 3 x 5 piece of paper. Include with your entry the hand printed words "Indulge A Little Sweepstakes." Mail your entry to: Indulge A Little Sweepstakes, P.O. Box 1397, Buffalo, NY 14269-1397. No mechanically reproduced entries accepted. Not responsible for late, lost, misdirected mail, or printing errors.

2. Three winners, one per month (Sept. 30, 1989, October 31, 1989 and November 30, 1989), will be selected in random drawings. All entries received prior to the drawing date will be eligible for that month's prize. This sweepstakes is under the supervision of MARDEN-KANE, INC. an independent judging organization whose decisions are final and binding. Winners will be notified by telephone and may be required to execute an affidavit of eligibility and release which must be returned within 14 days, or an alternate winner will be selected.

3. Prizes: 1st Grand Prize (1) a trip for two to Disneyworld in Orlando, Florida. Trip includes round trip air transportation, hotel accommodations for seven days and six nights, plus up to $700 expense money (ARV $3,500). 2nd Grand Prize (1) a seven-night Chandris Caribbean Cruise for two includes transportation from nearest major airport, accommodations, meals plus up to $1,000 in expense money (ARV $4,300). 3rd Grand Prize (1) a ten-day Hawaiian holiday for two includes round trip air transportation for two, hotel accommodations, sightseeing, plus up to $1,200 in spending money (ARV $7,700). All trips subject to availability and must be taken as outlined on the entry form.

4. Sweepstakes open to residents of the U.S. and Canada 18 years or older except employees and the families of Torstar Corp., its affiliates, subsidiaries and Marden-Kane, Inc. and all other agencies and persons connected with conducting this sweepstakes. All Federal, State and local laws and regulations apply. Void wherever prohibited or restricted by law. Taxes, if any are the sole responsibility of the prize winners. Canadian winners will be required to answer a skill testing question. Winners consent to the use of their name, photograph and/or likeness for publicity purposes without additional compensation.

5. For a list of prize winners, send a stamped, self-addressed envelope to Indulge A Little Sweepstakes Winners, P.O. Box 701, Sayreville, NJ 08871.

© 1989 HARLEQUIN ENTERPRISES LTD.

DL-SWPS

INDULGE A LITTLE—WIN A LOT!

Summer of '89 Subscribers-Only Sweepstakes

OFFICIAL ENTRY FORM

This entry must be received by: Sept. 30, 1989
This month's winner will be notified by: October 7, 1989
Trip must be taken between: Nov. 7, 1989–Nov. 7, 1990

YES, I want to win the Walt Disney World® vacation for two! I understand the prize includes round-trip airfare, first-class hotel, and a daily allowance as revealed on the "Wallet" scratch-off card.

Name ______________________________

Address ______________________________

City __________ State/Prov. ______ Zip/Postal Code ______

Daytime phone number ______________________________
Area code

Return entries with invoice in envelope provided. Each book in this shipment has two entry coupons—and the more coupons you enter, the better your chances of winning!

DINDL-1

INDULGE A LITTLE—WIN A LOT!

Summer of '89 Subscribers-Only Sweepstakes

OFFICIAL ENTRY FORM

This entry must be received by: Sept. 30, 1989
This month's winner will be notified by: October 7, 1989
Trip must be taken between: Nov. 7, 1989–Nov. 7, 1990

YES, I want to win the Walt Disney World® vacation for two! I understand the prize includes round-trip airfare, first-class hotel, and a daily allowance as revealed on the "Wallet" scratch-off card.

Name ______________________________

Address ______________________________

City __________ State/Prov. ______ Zip/Postal Code ______

Daytime phone number ______________________________
Area code

Return entries with invoice in envelope provided. Each book in this shipment has two entry coupons—and the more coupons you enter, the better your chances of winning!

© 1989 HARLEQUIN ENTERPRISES LTD.

DINDL-1